The Dagger Before Me

Heather Haven

The Wives of Bath Press

www.thewivesofbath.com

This book is a work of fiction. Characters, names, places, events, and incidents either are the product of the author's imagination or are used fictitiously, and any resemblance to any actual persons, living or dead, events, or locales is entirely coincidental.

The Wives of Bath Press
223 Vincent Drive
Mountain View, CA 94041

http:// www.thewivesofbath.com

Edited by Baird Nuckolls
Layout and book production by
Heather Haven and Baird Nuckolls

Print ISBN ISBN-13:978-0-9884086-5-4 (The Wives of Bath Press)
eBook ISBN -13:978-0-9884086-6-1 (The Wives of Bath Press)
First eBook edition August, 2012 (Books We Love)

Testimonials

"Percy is a great character, and I found myself smiling and laughing at her antics throughout the story. Anyone looking for a fun, fast read should certainly give this book a try. I know I'll be on the lookout for more about Percy and her adventures." Long and Short Reviews

"If you like to take a chance on a book, you won't be disappointed with this one. I am looking forward to reading her next book about Persephone Cole" Amazon Reader

The Persephone Cole Vintage Mystery Series:

*The Dagger Before Me - Book One
**Iced Diamonds - Book Two

*Formerly *Persephone Cole and the Halloween Curse*
**Formerly *Persephone Cole and the Christmas Killings Conundrum*

Dedication

This book is dedicated to my mother, Mary Lee, an original thinker if there ever was one; husband, Norman Meister, who loves strong women; and gutsy broads everywhere who get out there, do what they love, and blaze the trail for the rest of us.

Acknowledgments

I could never do any of this without my writing buddies, in particular, Baird Nuckolls, whose expertise in all things hold me in good stead. Thanks, too, to Robert Goldberg and Jeff Monaghan for help with the cover art.

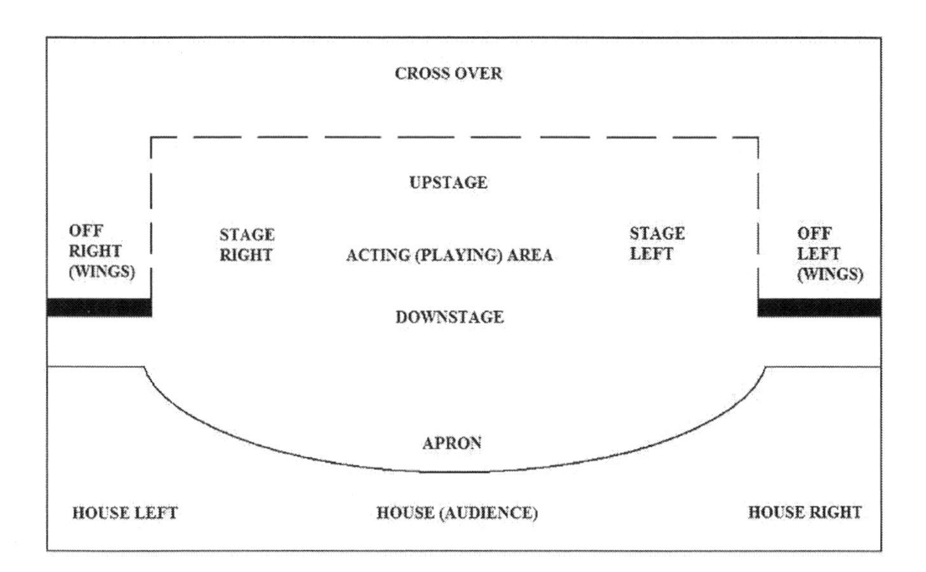
CROSS OVER
UPSTAGE
OFF
RIGHT
(WINGS)
STAGE
RIGHT
ACTING (PLAYING) AREA
STAGE
LEFT
OFF
LEFT
(WINGS)
DOWNSTAGE
APRON
HOUSE LEFT
HOUSE (AUDIENCE)
HOUSE RIGHT

Royal Theatre
Presents
The Tragedy of Macbeth

Chapter One

Persephone Cole's hand hovered over the ringing telephone. Waiting for the third ring was almost too much effort, like everything else in this heat, but Percy had a thing about answering a phone on the first ring. Sucking in a hot, sticky breath, she was ever aware of the oppressive temperature. She dripped with it. Eight-thirty-five a.m., eighty-three degrees, and climbing. Humidity high enough to wash your socks in. Welcome to Indian summer on the lower east side, one of the hottest ever recorded.

Percy reached over and turned off her only source of moving air, a small, beat-up oscillating fan that sounded like her eight-year old son's bike the time he put a clothespin on the spokes of the back wheel. Looking up at the wall, her gaze focused on her newly framed private investigator's license, barely a week old.

New York State Department of Licensing,
Private Investigator, Persephone Cole
Effective Date: October 15, 1942

Pride filled her at being one of New York City's first female P.I.s, instead of merely a secretary. Of course, technically she was both now, but a little extra work never scared Percy. She took a slug of tepid water - no ice to spare in weather like this -- and picked up the receiver. She pushed back in her chair, lifted and crossed her legs, resting them on a corner of the desk. She'd relax if it killed her.

"Good morning," she said, going into professional work mode. "Cole Investigations, Persephone Cole, private investigator speaking."

There was a beat, where both parties were silent. Then a male voice asked on the other end of the line,

"Is this Cole Investigations?"

That's what I said, bub. "Yes sir, it is."

"Who's this?" The voice was gruff, almost rude.

What are you, deaf? "This is Persephone Cole, private investigator."

"You sound like a woman." He barely disguised his astonishment.

And you sound like an ass. "That's right. This is Persephone Cole, private investigator for Cole Investigations."

She pulled her crossed legs off the desk, and leaned forward, her large, five foot-eleven inch frame causing the chair to creak in protest. Strands of long, flaming red hair broke free of the rubber band atop her head, damp locks sticking to her forehead and neck. Everything stuck to everything in weather like this.

"How may I help you?" She tried to keep her voice sweet. It was an effort.

"You can help me by handing the phone over to a man. Who's there? Give me Gil or Pop Cole."

"Gilleathain is deceased and Pop is out of the office on a long-term assignment."

"Crap."

"Uh-huh. So can I do something for you or not?" *If you hang up, you might just be turning down the best 'man' for the job. Put that in your pipe and smoke it.*

He let out a long hissing sigh, as if parceling out his breath in accordance with his thought processes. Percy blew down the front of her blouse waiting for him to either hang up or tell her what the hell he wanted. The cast iron phone felt like it weighed a ton, and if this was a big venture into 'no thanks' land, she'd just as soon end it now and get it over with. There was some grub in the kitchen with her name on it.

I'm starving. Oatmeal and canned peaches with diluted condensed milk ain't doing it for me. Maybe there's something else. Even Spam sounds pretty good right now.

While he thought, she pulled out the ever present sack of pistachios from the pocket of her trousers and threw it on the table. Still holding the earpiece with one hand, she rooted around inside the bag with the other. She popped a nut into her mouth and separated the meat from the shell with her teeth.

"Very well," he finally said. "I don't have time to try to find another agency, if there is one. Besides, from what I understand,
every available man seems to be tied up or drafted. It's such a nuisance."

"The war's a hassle, but don't let it get you down." She picked the shells out of her mouth, continuing to chew the nut as silently as possible.

If he heard what she said, he ignored her comment. "I knew the Cole Brothers from when I was starting out years ago. The boys helped me once before and they were honest. Are you honest?"

"I can be."

"I guess it'll have to be you, God help me. My name is Dexter Wainwright. You know who I am, little lady?"

"I do. You're a hotshot Broadway producer and you can call me Miss Cole. Now we got the introductions out of the way, what can I do for you?"

"Last night one of my actors fell from the overhead catwalk and broke his neck. He's dead."

"That's too bad. I hope he had an understudy," Percy added.

Clearly taken aback, Dexter Wainwright gurgled. "No. Yes. What? Yes, of course, but that's not why I'm calling."

"Then get to it." She popped another pistachio into her mouth.

"The police don't believe it was an accident. They want to close my whole show down. It's the...ah...Scottish play. Maybe you've seen it? We've been in previews for the last four weeks."

Like I have a buck-fifty to throw away on your show. "No, I haven't, but I've read about it in the papers. Macbeth, right?"

"Uh-huh." He grunted. "It happened sometime around midnight. I don't know what the hell Carlisle was doing in the theatre at that time of night."

"Getting himself killed, for one thing."

"I have until eight o'clock tonight to find some answers or the police are threatening to lock the doors." He paused for a moment. "You know, I think you might be a wiseacre."

Percy let out a chuckle. "Could be, but like you say, everybody else is drafted or tied up. If you want me, it's the going rate, fifteen bucks a day plus expenses. You got that?"

"Got it."

"Good. You're at the Royal Theatre, right?"

"Right."

"I'll be there in an hour. And Mr. Wainwright..."

"Yes?"

"When I get there, you're going to tell me the truth. All of it."

"I...I..."

Percy hung up on a stuttering Broadway producer.

Chapter Two

Elsie, you were right. Since we dare not be seen together, this is the perfect place to leave messages for one another. No one will suspect a thing. I received a letter yesterday about father's estate. After death taxes, debts, and mamma's illness and funeral, there is nothing left. You and I are on our own. I saw one of the warning missives you sent out and it was cleverly done. From now on, no more warnings, dear sister; we will simply do. Wainwright will pay. They will all pay. I miss you.

Evelyn

Chapter Three

Percy blew an errant wet curl off her forehead, and left the parlor, office, carrying the empty water glass. She trudged down the long hallway of the railroad apartment on the lower east side she and her son shared with her mother, father, and much younger sister, Sera.

Sera's real name was Serendipity, named after arriving unexpectedly fifteen years following the first two children spaced one year apart. Percy's older brother, Adjudication, married and became a lawyer, no doubt influenced by his given name. Stuck with Adjudication, Persephone, and Serendipity, the three Cole offspring went by the nicknames of Jude, Percy, and Sera, except to parents who called them by their given names.

Pop's Christian name was Habakkuk, for the biblical prophet. Everyone called him Pop. Mother's was Lamentation. Everyone called her Mother. When these two met, their first names convinced everyone who knew them, theirs would be a marriage made in heaven. Forty-three years later that was still true. Percy christened her eight-year old son, Oliver, putting a minor chink in the Cole family tradition of odd first names. She hoped.

Percy pushed the swinging kitchen door open and went inside. Mother sat at the table, peeling and cutting up potatoes. Her long, untamed white hair was contained for once, twisted and clipped off her face and neck in the heat. Worn down as a rule, people often remarked that between her wild hair, thin body, and daffy personality, she reminded them of a Dandelion caught in a windstorm. Naturally, this was not said in the woman's presence.

Persephone looked at the woman who bore her with great affection. "Mother, you'd never know by looking at you the east coast is in the grip of a killer heat wave from Florida to Maine. And in the middle of October."

"There you are, Persephone." Mother gave her a bright smile. "If you're taking a break from the office, come help me peel potatoes. Your father wants potato salad tonight. I think I remember the recipe." Her shoulders hunched over, as if burdened by a sudden thought.

"Oh, dear, I can't recall if it's two pounds of potatoes or two pounds of fresh dill. I was thinking of throwing in some parsnips. They're white, too. You don't suppose it's two pounds of mayonnaise, do you? No," she answered herself. "That would be too runny."

"My money's on the potatoes, Mother. Work with that. I'd scratch the parsnips, if I was you."

"Oh, dear, I have so many of them and they'll just go bad."

"Any cold sodas left in the fridge?"

"You might check, dear. It's hard to keep them around with so many of Serendipity's gentlemen callers."

"Guzzle them right down, do they?" Percy crossed the worn linoleum of the large kitchen floor and faced the old refrigerator, the top cooling coils vibrating more than usual. The morning sun streamed through the large, paned-glass window facing a courtyard four stories below.

"Jeesh, it already feels like a steam bath in here." Percy moved from the refrigerator to the window, and pulled down the aging shade. "That's better."

"I'm worried about your father, Persephone." Mother stopped her peeling. "Twelve-hour shifts, working all night trying to catch these vandals. He never does sleep right during the day. Destroying the Lord's house is not a nice thing to do. I don't care if you are an atheist. Or is it agnostic? I can never remember which one is what. What they need is a little faith." She shook her head and clucked her tongue, picking up the paring knife again.

"I think the problem is too much faith, Mother, coupled with strong feelings of self-righteousness. Then they start swinging a pickaxe. Pop won't be doing the job much longer, anyway. He said the rabbis are pulling the plug next week on the project. Running out of money. But we'll be okay. I just got a client, and I plan to get a lot more." Percy opened the refrigerator door. She clucked her tongue, as well, but for another reason. "This stupid thing is almost as warm inside as it is out. I know this is your pride and joy, Mother --"

"Your father got it for me brand new, Persephone," her mother interrupted. "It was the only present I ever wanted, a nineteen twenty-seven Monitor Top refrigerator. And we were the first ones on the block, too."

"And now it needs to be fixed."

"Maybe, but I'm not keeping anything perishable in there, Persephone. I'm using the Schlitz cooler in the corner by the larder."

"So what is this, a glorified closet? We should unplug it. Save ourselves the noise and electricity."

"If you wish, dear. Serendipity is bringing more ice on her way home from work for the cooler. She's working half a day."

"Before she runs off to an air-conditioned movie. That's the only date she'll go on these days." Percy reached down and pulled the plug out of the wall socket. The kitchen fell into an agreeable silence.

"She does like it when the boys take her to an air-cooled movie house. I've never been to one myself. I wonder how they chill the air? It must be done with ice. Did you say you have a client?" Mother stopped peeling potatoes again and looked at her eldest daughter.

"I did. I have. Is there any fruit around? I'm hungry."

"On the table." Mother pointed to a bowl in the center. "What kind of a job?"

Percy glanced into the fruit bowl. "Oh, not these old apples again." She picked one up, took a bite, and made a face. "I swear, this batch came over on the Mayflower. Where is all the fresh fruit these days?"

"The best pickings go to our boys overseas. You know that, my dear. You're just enjoying yourself complaining."

"Along with the best dairy, meat, and vegetables." Percy mumbled, as if her mother hadn't spoken. "Except for potatoes and rice. That's why I'm shaped like the Hindenburg, not because I can't control myself. It's the war's fault I'm fat," Percy joked.

"Persephone, dear, don't you say that about yourself. You're not fat."

"Thank you, Mother."

"You're zaftig."

"Thank you, Mother."

"Such a sad day for the airship industry when that beautiful ship caught fire." Mother looked away, musing. "After that you couldn't ride one at all; they just went away. Poof! I've always wanted to, you know, ride in an airship. Float through the air like a bird." She continued peeling potatoes and throwing them into a bowl of water. "Tell me about your new client, dear. Is it more secretarial work? Not that it surprises me someone else would want to hire you. You are very good at organizing an office. You've done wonders for your father's filing system, but --"

"I'm going to cut you off at the pass, Mother. You're beginning to wander, and I've got to leave for midtown sometime this century. No secretarial work. Detecting, Mother, and don't tell Pop."

"Persephone, you know how your father feels --"

"Yeah, well, too bad," Percy interrupted, taking another bite of the apple. "Mother, I'm thirty-five years old. Three. five. In five more years I'll be forty. I don't have to tell you, time passes like that." She snapped her fingers.

"That's what calendars are for, dear." Mother's tone was one of cheer, coupled with imparting helpful information. "So we can keep track. I can get you one, if you like."

Percy knelt down in front of the older woman. "Mother, what I really mean is I been working for Cole Investigations for seventeen years. I helped Pop and Uncle Gil solve a lot of cases, too, between us chickens."

"Your father always said you were a big help."

"Now I want to be out there doing it for myself. I'm tired of sitting behind a desk answering a phone and saying, 'Cole Investigations, may I help you?' I want to *be* Cole Investigations...along with Pop, of course. It took me eighteen months of studying nights and weekends to get the P.I. license. And I paid two hard-earned bucks for it. Now I got the chance. Percy Cole has a brain, and she wants to use it."

"That's lovely, Persephone, just lovely. You have such a way with words."

"But will they work on Pop?"

"I wouldn't count on it, dear." Mother shook her head. "You know your father, once he makes up his mind. What are you going to be doing, Persephone? I hope it isn't dangerous. You have a young son to think about."

"Naw. A cake walk, Mother. A little trip uptown to a Broadway theatre, talk to the producer, and head on home. You'll never even know I'm gone."

Big words, toots, but what the hell.

"I still don't think your father will be happy." Mother mused again then picked up a potato and dug out one of the eyes with the knife.

"That's why we won't tell him. Besides, I haven't been paid by Cole Investigation for three weeks. Why? No moola. I'll bring in fifteen bucks a day doing this. Pop's only getting five a day and he won't see any of that 'til the job's over. But that's Brooklyn for you."

"Fifteen dollars," Mother said in awe. "In a day! My, my, my. And this sack of potatoes only cost three cents," she said looking at the ten-pound bag. "Of course, it was on sale."

"Fifteen bucks a day can buy a lot of potatoes." Percy pressed her advantage. "And I plan to parlay this into a few days, at least. Oliver could use a new pair of shoes soon. He's almost outgrown his last pair. Where is he, anyway?" She looked around the kitchen.

"He's at his cub scout meeting. Then you promised he could spend the afternoon at little Freddy's house making teepees out of popsicle sticks and working on their Halloween costumes. The boys are going to walk straight there after the meeting. I think Oliver wants to be the Green Lantern."

"Maybe I can talk him into going as the Sheik of Araby. That's only a headband around your face on an old white sheet. Unless you're willing to make his costume, Mother. You sew so beautifully. I love that new robe you made me."

"You can save your sweet talk, Persephone Cole. I already told the boy I would make it for him."

"Thanks. And in return I promise to take care of the refrigerator, scout's honor." She held up two fingers. "I'll give Sylvia a call later just to make sure everything's okay with Oliver." She tapped her forehead. "I've got her number somewhere around here."

"The phone number is on the side of the refrigerator." Mother pointed with the paring knife.

"Well there, you see? I was wrong." Percy raised her hands to the ceiling in praise. "This broken-down piece of crap *still* has a purpose." She went to the myriad of papers taped or held to the surface by magnets on the side of the fridge and started searching. "Got it! Murray Hill four-seven-seven-three."

"What is her last name?" Mother, closed her eyes and concentrated. "Rendell. Sylvia Rendell. Such a lovely young woman. She asked for my recipe for split pea soup. Her mother was one of the Pipsmeyers over in Great Neck. No one ever asked me for a recipe before. She's gone now."

"Sylvia's mother, right? Not Sylvia."

"Sylvia couldn't ask for my split pea recipe if she had passed over, now could she? And you a detective with a certificate and everything," Mother chided.

"Just trying to keep it clear."

"Sylvia's husband is overseas somewhere in the Pacific. They can never tell you exactly where, can they? I think her father lives with them. Here, not the Pacific. He used to be in plumbing --"

"Hold that thought, Mother," Percy interrupted. "You can fill me in later. I've got to go change into work clothes and hop on the BMT. I told this guy I'd be there in an hour."

Percy bumped the kitchen door with the side of her shoulder, setting it on an outward swing, and passed through. She stopped, held the door open, and wheeled around to face her mother.

"And remember, mum's the word to Pop on what I'm doing for now. I'll call you later. I'll try to get some decent fruit when I'm in midtown, something that doesn't have as many wrinkles as Winston Churchill's face. They've got a few good farmers' markets in Hell's Kitchen. And thanks for pointing me in the right direction for the phone number; Murray Hill four-seven-seven-three," she repeated, trying to memorize the number. "And tell Pop I'm taking his number two fedora." Her mind flashed to his thick, silver hair, often covered by one of two favored hats.

"Did you lose your hairbrush, again, Persephone?"

"Yes, ma'am, and no time to search for it." The doorbell rang. "Someone's at the door, Mother. I'll get it."

Percy ran down the hallway, looked out the peephole, and swung the door wide open for the downstairs neighbor and friend, Rachel Goldberg.

"Mrs. Goldberg." Percy's tone was warm but hurried. "Come on in. Mother's in the kitchen. I need to get dressed and go see a new client."

"A client, Persela?" Short and tubby, head topped with salt and pepper-hair, good-hearted Mrs. Goldberg spoke with a heavy Yiddish accent. She was the only person in the world to call Percy 'Persela'. It was a term of endearment from a family friend that had known Percy since she was a small child. She clapped her hands together in delight.

"So go! Who's stopping you? Get on those clothes and see if you can make somebody happy with your detecting business, such a thing for a young lady to do, but if someone has to do it, Persela, it might as well be you, because you are such a clever girl, always with the thinking and the looking at things like nobody else does and who found my wallet, which I accidentally threw down the laundry chute all those years ago." Mrs. Goldberg finally stopped talking in her run-on sentence and took a deep breath.

"I am here to try to teach your mother to make latkes like I promised, but she doesn't want to make them with potatoes. She says parsnips because they are in the larder and they are going bad! Did you ever hear of such a thing?"

"Well, you know Mother, Mrs. Goldberg." Percy laughed lightly, as she turned and opened the door to her bedroom. "You've been trying to teach her to cook for years and you see where it's got you."

"Oy! Not years, bubala, decades." Mrs. Goldberg hollered to her. "Decades I've been trying to teach that woman to cook, as if I have nothing better to do with my time and my

Henny wasn't a man waiting for his own dinner, God bless him for waiting and never saying a word --"

"Mother's in the kitchen. Go on in," Percy interrupted, pointing down the hall, as she closed the door to her room behind her.

"Oy!" Percy leaned against the door, sounding a little like Mrs. Goldberg. "Sometimes it's hard to get out of this place."

Chapter Four

It's working, Evelyn, just like you said. The show is coming to a halt. I've been practicing throwing the knife when no one is around. I'll try to throw one during the show, if I can get away with it. Even if it doesn't strike Sir Anthony, someone else will be hit. There are so many of them onstage, someone's bound to see the blade of Macbeth's dagger coming at them. I know I mustn't feel so wicked. We're only doing what needs to be done. Right is on our side. I miss you, too, so very much.

Elsie

Chapter Five

Percy climbed up the subway stairs at Forty-second Street and Seventh Avenue, better known as Times Square. Ordinarily she enjoyed this part of the City, so different from the lower east side. Midtown Manhattan pulsed with energetic, stylish people, going here and there in their late-model cars or scurrying along the sidewalks on well-shod feet. Percy liked to observe this condensed part of city life. It was a study in human nature like no other.

The overheated subway had smelled of urine and sweat. Along with all the other bodies, she emerged from the bowels of the City looking for fresh air. What she found was broiling hot streets and sidewalks, littered with piles of garbage and trash. Gusts of scorching air from the exhausts of passing vehicles blew bits of rubbish around, the only moving air in this hot spell.

What a time for the teamsters to pull a garbage strike, as if the City doesn't stink enough.

She threw the dark blue jacket of her pants suit over the other arm of her damp, tailored blouse, allowing the previously covered arm some cooling off time. Adjusting Pop's fedora over the red curls piled on top of her head, she pulled the brim forward to shield her face from a remorseless sun. Masses of tourists, civilians, and soldiers jousted with her for space on the crowded sidewalks the four short blocks to Forty-Sixth Street.

Arriving at the Royal theatre, a large marquis overhead announced the previews of Shakespeare's Macbeth. The marquis featured a stark black and white drawing of the face of what some people considered one of Britain's finest Shakespearian actors, the newly knighted Sir Anthony Slattery. Sir Anthony's strong features were surrounded by smaller caricatures of people brandishing swords and archaic weaponry, all looking grim and murderous.

Strategically placed bright red lettering used words like "brilliant" "riveting" and "wonderful" followed by lots of exclamation points. Similar posters were plastered everywhere possible on the building's façade.

Percy pulled out a ripped newspaper clipping on New York City theatres from her pocket and read. The Royal Theatre was one of the last bastions of the golden age of theatre, having been built in the late eighteen hundreds. At that time, productions included not only straight plays and musicals, but operas, as well. The theatre's proscenium arch, which framed the stage, was close to forty-feet high, accommodating the most opulent of operas. Reportedly, Aida marched two elephants onstage, plus a cast of eighty. Eleonora Duse, Sarah Bernhardt, Enrico Caruso were just a few of the performers who flocked here to be a part of its magic. So did the audiences. Seating capacity was fifteen hundred people.

Jeesh, fifteen hundred people in one place eight times a week. That's a lot of hoi polloi.

The front of the theatre was closed and locked, it being nine-thirty in the morning. Percy looked for a side entrance and found a narrow alleyway. She walked down it noting the trash piled high on one side. A slender fledgling tree fought for survival amidst the rubble. Three quarters of the way in, there was a door with an overhead sign marked, 'stage entrance'. Percy shrugged into her jacket then pulled on the handle only to discover it was locked. She rapped on the metal door, and it sprung open immediately.

An old man stood on the other side of the door, sparse grey whiskers sprouting here and there on an unshaven, sad face. A hat similar to the one Percy pilfered from Pop's hat rack sat atop his head, but more faded and beat up. He looked her up and down.

"You're a big one. You that detective lady?"

"I am. You that stage door Johnny?"

"Very funny." His voice had a disapproving edge to it. "Everybody's got a wise crack around here. I'm Ned. Mr. Wainwright is waiting for you in his office." He gestured with his thumb. "Third door to the left."

Ned flattened his body along the wall to let her pass. Percy stepped up the one tread into the theatre. She paused for a moment, allowing her eyes to adjust to the dark, so different from the merciless glare of the unrelenting sun. The air, too, was different,
cooler, but stagnant and ancient, reeking of old ropes, dust, and gears.

To the right was a small booth carved into the wall. A Dutch door wearing a sturdy lock had the top half open to reveal a wall lined with tiny, numbered square cubicles. Each cubicle held a matching numbered key. In front of the cubicles, a single weathered wooden barstool sat, a messy newspaper tossed on top.

The man reached around her, undid the latch on the lower half of the door, and pushed. He passed through, picked up the newspaper and sat down, scrupulously ignoring her.

"I'm glad I don't have your job. I don't think I could get in there." Ned grunted but did not look up from his papers. "So, Ned, tell me what's your schedule? How many hours a day do you sit here?"

He looked up into her face, wariness coloring his features. "The theatre's open, I'm here. Nobody supposed to be here without someone at the stage door. Them's the rules."

"Were you here last night at midnight?"

He pointed an arthritic, twisted finger at her. "I knew you was going to try to blame me for this. I done nothing. Got no call to. I just sit here and mind my own business."

"Ned, you misunderstand me." Percy crooned, leaning into the small room and bathing him in a warm smile. "No one's blaming you for anything. I just wanted to know if you'd seen anything when you were here."

"Whatever I seen, I told the coppers."

"Good. That's good. You mind your business, sure, but you're a smart man. You see everybody coming and going. I could use your help, that's all."

"My help?" He looked up at her, mystified.

"Sure. You see what's what. I need that." She reached inside her pocket, pulled out three one-dollar bills, fanned them out, and laid them on the top of the narrow shelf of the Dutch door.

Ned dropped the newspaper to the floor. He looked up at her, his face breaking out into a toothy, yellow grin.

"Maybe I can help you, lady." He preened. "There's a lot to see around here, and I sees it. Not much gets by me; that's the truth." His hand slipped over the fanned bills.

Percy opened her mouth to speak, but heard a deep, base voice calling out from inside the darkened theatre.

"Miss Cole, are you out there? I thought I heard someone knock on the door. I've been waiting for you."

"That's Wainwright." Ned whispered and pulled back into his booth. "You'd better go. He's not always the most pleasant of fellows."

Percy nodded. "I'll catch you later, Ned." She started down the hall.

"You know where I'll be," he called after her.

She glanced back, as Ned picked up the money. She smiled; he winked. He was her new pal.

The detective continued down a narrow hallway wearing a mish-mash of neutral colors. Splatters of beige, grey, white, and yellow paint covered irregular walls, walls plastered and re-plastered many times. What color the interior was supposed to be was difficult to say.

I'm going with drab.

Near the ceiling, low wattage bulbs, protected from breakage by steel mesh screens, were screwed into wall sockets every five feet or so, and provided a minimum of light. In between, eighteen by twenty-four inch posters, encased in dusty glass, showed previous productions, some dating back to the turn of the century.

If she hadn't been summoned by the commanding voice and saw the shadow of an imposing man standing in a door frame, she would have stopped and read a few. Even someone from a non-theatrical background such as she, knew the importance of New York City's Royal Theatre. It was legend.

The man hovering in the doorway, probably in his late forties, was tall even by her standards. Dressed in a three-piece pinstriped, charcoal gray suit that fit impeccably, white shirt and deep red tie, he had a certainty about his place in the world. This was a man used to being obeyed and believed his existence counted, probably more than most. Percy was on her guard from the first minute she saw him.

"Mr. Wainwright?" She approached him in the door way and extended her hand. "I'm Persephone Cole."

She wasn't sure if he would take her hand or turn away. It would tell her a lot, his initial gesture, so she measured his reaction to her carefully.

"Miss Cole." He gripped her hand in his, holding it for a brief moment, then shook it. A smile broke out on his face, which transformed it instantly from cold and imposing to warm and compelling. Beautiful, even white teeth were set in a strong face with a Dick Tracy jaw line. "Dexter Wainwright. Thank you for coming on such short notice."

Percy fought to keep herself in check. He was as handsome as any leading actor she'd seen on the silver screen and a good four inches taller than she. It was novel, looking up to someone not standing on a stepladder. Plus, she wasn't completely sure how to deal with this man who could turn charm, intelligence, and animal appeal on and off at will.

"Yeah, hey, so I'm here." *Oh, grand, Percy. Good going. Clever repartee and all that.*

"Please come in." If he found her reply to be wanting, he didn't indicate it.

The producer gave her hand a small tug and pulled her into the small white office. Percy looked around at a room that contained mismatched office furniture in what had once been a dressing room for several people. Naked bulbs surrounding six large make-up mirrors on all four sides provided lighting for the room. Side by side and evenly spaced apart, the mirrors hung above one long makeup table bolted to the wall. A desk, chairs, and two filing cabinets were shoved haphazardly into the remaining area.

Another man in his late twenties or early thirties sat at one end of the makeup table, studying a thick mound of papers clipped together in one corner. He raised his head, an appraising look coming into his eyes as he saw her. With slicked back, sandy brown hair and soft brown eyes, he had an easy smile.

He, too, wore a crisp white shirt, but there was no jacket in sight. The shirt sleeves were rolled up, giving an air of casualness, but were precise in their uniformity. Collar turned up, the starched shirt's top three buttons were open to the man's chest, once again suggesting a studied casualness.

Around the waist of his black cuffed trousers, a patterned gray, yellow, and blue tie ran through the belt loops instead of a belt, finished off in a square knot.

Percy had seen something like that worn by Fred Astaire in a movie once. It looked as odd to her then as it did now. In fact, she wouldn't have been surprised if the man before her leapt up and

began to tap dance, breaking into a Cole Porter song. Instead, he turned to her with a questioning look on his face.

"Are you here for the tall witch's part, luv?" Unlike Dexter Wainwright, he spoke with a clipped British accent. "You're going to have to lose a few pounds first, dearie. Sorry, but do come back after that. Yours is an interesting face."

"Ah, Miss Cole." Dexter Wainwright stepped in between them. "This is our illustrious big-mouth director, Hugo Cranston." He turned to the director. "Hugo, this is the private detective I've hired to find some answers to the problems the production's been having."

Cranston shot the producer a sideways look of surprise. "A lady dick? Cor blimey, I never heard of such a thing." He stood up, stared into her face, and extended his hand.

"Then you need to get around more, Mr. Cranston," Percy said, shaking his hand firmly. "We're out there."

Sure, maybe I'm the only one you and I have heard of, but there has to be a few more scattered across this great nation of ours.

"Then I stand corrected, Miss Cole." He gave a short bow. "I like the look. Very Marlene Dietrich, although with those eyes, I'd stick to green. I'll leave you both to it. I have auditions soon, anyway." The director dropped her hand and threw her a warm, genuine smile. He moved to the door, pausing for a moment. "I jest not about your face, Miss Cole. When and if you should drop a few pounds..." He stopped speaking but looked her up and down.

"Gotcha. Should I find myself coming out of an eight-month coma, you're going to be the first person I call."

Hugo Cranston tossed his head back and gave off a hearty laugh. She could hear the sound of it resonating as he walked away. Despite his backhanded compliment, Percy liked him.

"Sit down, Miss Cole."

The American producer pointed to a chair. Percy remained standing.

"Want a Coke?" Without waiting for an answer, he opened the door of a small refrigerator kept under the makeup table and took out two bottles. He reached for a church key and pried the caps off, while Percy gaped at the small appliance.

"That little thing is a refrigerator?"

"Yes, brand new. Paid a king's ransom for it, but I'm here at the theatre for hours at a time and I like having cold sodas in my
office." He handed her one and took a long pull off his bottle. She watched him for a moment then did the same. After he swallowed,
he went on. "You'll have to forgive my Limey friend, Hugo. He doesn't always --"

"Forget it, Wainwright. We've got more important things to talk about than perceived insults. Thanks for the Coke."

"Good." He looked relieved and sat down. She dropped into a chair across from him. He leaned forward, elbows on his knees, and looked into her eyes. "I want you to know, you impressed me on the phone."

"Did I?"

"Yes, that part where you said I had to tell you 'all of it' when you got here. How did you know there was more to this than Carlisle's tragic fall?"

"The cops don't threaten to close down a show after one death, even if it's suspected foul play. And you've been in previews in this theatre for nearly a month. That's a long time.

Usually, there are pre-Broadway tryouts, Boston, Philadelphia, some place like that, to work out the bugs. Then the show hits Broadway doing previews for maybe a week, two weeks tops. It's an expensive proposition the way you're doing it."

The producer raised his eyebrows in appreciation. "Do you have a theatrical background, Miss Cole?"

She shook her head. "I read a lot."

"You're right about most of it. Carlisle was only one of a string of accidents we've been having. All serious but nothing's been fatal until last night. You know about the Scottish play?"

"Macbeth? Sure. It's --"

"Shhhh," he interrupted, adding to the shush of his words with a wave of his hands. He pushed the air currents around him, as if warding off cigarette smoke or something evil. "We don't say the name. We only say it when performing the play; when the lines dictate."

"You're putting me on. You never use the word 'Macbeth' otherwise?"

"Will you stop that?" Fear tinged his annoyance. "Listen, I didn't believe in the Curse, either, until we started rehearsals, but I'm convinced now, believe you me."

"I still think you're putting me on." Percy's voice was riddled with doubt.

"I wish I was." He rose and began to pace the small, narrow room. "We were supposed to have opened two weeks ago, but cast

members keep getting sick or hurt or just plain dropping out. We need to keep rehearsing just to bring the new ones up to speed. First our leading lady, Felicity Dowell bowed out."

"That would be Lady Mac--"

"Shhhh! Don't. Say. The. Name." Wainwright emphasized each word individually.

Percy laughed. "Okay, no names. Why did she bow out?"

"She got food poisoning the day after we arrived in New York and was almost run down by a truck three days later. She says the driver was coming right at her. Then she got a threatening letter. Her agent gave us the bad news the following day. Last week a twenty-five pound sandbag fell from one of the flies and nearly killed our stage manager. As it is, the weight of it crushed his shoulder. If he had been standing a little more to the left, he'd be dead. Carl's going to be in the hospital for a long time. He may never be able to use his arm again."

"You said there were other people who dropped out. Who are they?"

"You mean aside from our leading lady? A spear carrier, the gentlewoman, and one of the witches, all called in saying they weren't coming back. Unlike most productions of the Bard's play, this one has the witches in the background of nearly every scene, silently casting their spells. We're playing up the curse of the Scotsman to the hilt, as if he has no control over what he does."

"Sort of Halloween meets Shakespeare. Any black cats?" Percy kept a straight face, although it was tough.

"We thought of it." If he noticed Percy's humorous take on the subject, he didn't indicate it. "We even considered using Sir Anthony's own cat, but he's not black. Anyway, that's why Hugo asked you about the witch audition. She's very important. We have one witch of normal height, one really tall and one very short. It's Hugo's idea of a sight gag. He's a good director for all his ridiculousness."

"Can actors drop out like that? Don't they have a contract?"

"A good agent can get you out of any contract. That said, performers don't usually walk out on a show. There are

so few jobs out there, when they get one they tend to stay no matter what. Some
of these people came across the pond to do the show. I've never seen anything like this."

"What about the three who legged it? They come over from England?"

"No, they were doing lesser parts. We picked them up here in the states. Two called to have us forward their paychecks. One hasn't even done that. That's why I don't get this. It's like the cast has got the willies or something. You'll see it. You'll see how they behave. Like we're cursed."

"Give me the names of those three. I'm going to pay them a visit. Actually, I'd like a cast list."

Wainwright nodded but his mind was elsewhere. He didn't answer but chewed on his thumbnail for awhile, deep in thought.

Percy watched him in silence then said, "I can tell there's more. Let's have it."

He studied her for a moment, walked back to the chair, and sat. He leaned into her and touched the top of her hand lightly with his. His face broke out into what Percy liked to think of as the 'used vacuum cleaner salesman' smile.

"I don't know if you're aware of all the aspects of what a producer does, Miss Cole. Ah, may I call you Persephone?"

"No, but go on."

His smile faltered then he rallied instantly. "It's not just the job of finding backers, but often on new projects, we work with the playwright, the composer, even the lyricist on development. Sometimes this process can take months or even years."

"You're being evasive. What has this got to do with Shakespeare?"

"Nothing, nothing. I'm just telling you sometimes there's more to a producer's job than meets the eye. Sometimes you make enemies."

"So sometimes you make enemies. Like who?"

He thought for a moment, opened his mouth to speak, but shook his head. There was a gentle knock on the door. The producer stood, walked a few feet, but ignored it.

"Nothing. It's nothing."

Percy studied him, and shook her head, setting her empty soda bottle on the counter. "I think you'd better give me an advance while I'm still willing to work for you. Then I'll need to look
around, meet some of the cast of characters. Got any papers from the cops? Something about Carlisle's death? What part did he play, anyway?"

"Macduff."

The knock came again, this time a little louder. Wainwright continued his ignoring routine.

"That's a big part." She looked over at the door.

"I see you know something about the play."

"Enough to get by. Who's your stage manager now? Can I speak to him?"

"The assistant stepped into the position, but I don't have anyone to fill his shoes yet. That's what I'm doing here. I've been wracking my brain, trying to come up with someone. And, of course, Broadway's a small community. Rumors are spreading like wild fires. Not many people want to work for us now."

The knock became more persistent. He still didn't respond.

"Get the door, Wainwright. Never know, might be something important."

"Come in." Wainwright didn't move but called out in a voice filled with exasperation.

The door opened slowly and an attractive young woman, brunette hair cut in the latest fashion, stuck her head in. Seeing only Wainwright standing near the door, a slow smile crossed her face.

"Hi, boss." Her voice radiated familiarity. "I didn't know if you were in here or not. Bad news. The Fire Marshall says we have to move the scenery from blocking the back exit. After that, I thought I'd run over to Schraffts and bring us back some breakfast."

"Ah, Mavis," the producer said and gestured to Percy. "This is Miss Persephone Cole. Miss Cole, Mavis Hewitt, my private secretary." Producer and assistant exchanged a look Percy couldn't quite place.

Percy nodded her head in a greeting. "Miss Hewitt." *And just how private is private, I wonder?*

The smiling girl, no older than twenty-two or twenty-three, stepped inside. She was tall, five- foot six or seven, slim, and dressed in a bias cut powder blue dress, more suited for an afternoon tea than working backstage in a theatre. The only sign she was a working girl was a clipboard she carried in her right hand, thick with well-used papers.

"Good morning, Miss Cole. Dexter, ah, Mr. Wainwright told me he hired you to find out why we're having so many accidents around here. Unlike everybody else, I don't think the bad luck we've been having has anything to do with our production of Macbeth."

Wainwright pointed a finger at the girl. "Don't say the name. Have you no respect?"

"I see you think this is all nonsense, Mavis." Percy smiled. "Why don't you tell me more about the curse associated with performing this play?"

"It's just a silly superstition, Miss Cole, centuries old." Mavis flipped her well-groomed curls in distain. "It has no more validity than throwing a hat on a bed or whistling in a dressing room. Many people in the theatre believe real spells are called upon when the three witches' scene is spoken. Then when you say the name 'Macbeth' off-stage, you invoke these spells, which can cause great harm. That's why it's taboo for actors and anyone involved in the play to even utter the name in or outside the theatre. It's referred to as the Scottish Play or Bard's Play. It's silly," she repeated with a superior air. Her face broke out in a likable smile.

Annoyed, Wainwright jumped in. "You can say what you like, Mavis, but something's going on around here. And people's beliefs are powerful. Don't dismiss it out of hand." She continued to look unabashed but shrugged amiably.

"Besides," he went on, "superstition is the reason I wanted to premier around Halloween with this production, to play on people's fanciful notions. Winchell's column mentions 'the curse' nearly every day. We're trying to use it to our advantage. But we've got to open soon. As for the actual curse, there may be something to it; there may not be, as you say, but it has to be stopped. I need to talk to the Fire Marshall."

Wainwright crossed to the door. Without looking at the girl, he threw an order to her, his voice filled with impatience. "Cut a check for forty-five dollars for Miss Cole." He turned back to Percy. "A three-day advance should be sufficient, shouldn't it?"

"Yeah, sure." Percy was barely able to keep from stammering.

Forty-five smackers in advance! We eat tonight!

"But I'm going to need some expense money, too." Percy's tone was easy, as if she did this every day.

"As you wish. She's asking for any paperwork we have from the police, too, Mavis." The producer waved his hand in a curt manner. "See that she gets five dollars from petty cash and I'll need receipts for that, Miss Cole. For God's sake let's try to get this
production back on track. I'm losing a fortune with all these postponements and recasts."

He walked out and slammed the door. Both women stared after him for a beat and then looked at one another.

"Big shot, huh," commented Percy.

"What's that?" Mavis asked with a smile.

"An important man."

"He's one of the country's leading producers. England's, too. They call him charismatic. Many stars will only work for him."

"Uh-huh. Who's the detective assigned to the case?" Percy took off Pop's fedora and fanned herself. "Man, it's hot."

"Yes, I know. I'm sorry. The cooling system isn't turned on until a half an hour before each performance, not that we get much of it back stage." Mavis pulled a silken hanky from her sleeve and blotted at her brow. "Although the radio says there's a cold front coming in from Canada sometime tonight. It should drop fifteen to twenty degrees, closer to normal."

"From your mouth to God's ears."

"Beg pardon?"

"Just a saying. Forget it."

The girl smiled and glanced down at the clipboard, lifting page after page until she came to the one she was looking for. "Ah, here it is. It's Detective Michael O'Malley."

O'Malley! Pop's beat partner from the old days. Maybe I'm catching a break on this.

"Detective O'Malley took a few items with him for which he gave me a receipt."

"Thanks. I'll give him a call. You want to write down the stuff he took? And while you're at it, give me a cast list and the names and addresses of the performers who hoofed it."

Mavis stared at her. "I beg your pardon?"

"Dropped out of the show, took off. You got a phone around here I can use?"

"Oh, I thought by 'hoofed' you meant a dancer. The only public phone backstage is hanging on the wall right outside the door, but you can use that one over there. Mr. Wainwright won't mind, I'm sure." Mavis pointed to a black telephone on the corner of a desk strewn with papers. "I'll make up a list for you now." She retreated to a small table in a corner, sat down, and began to write.

Percy hesitated. "Ah, could I have a little privacy for this call?"

Embarrassed, Mavis stood. "Of course. I'm sorry." She moved toward the door. "I'll come back with the list when I'm finished." She closed the door silently behind her.

Percy waited a beat and picked up the receiver, listened for a dial tone, and dialed zero.

"Operator, you want to give me the police station at midtown, south precinct? No, this is not an emergency." The dispatcher answered on the other end of the line, announcing the precinct with pride.

"Detective Michael O'Malley around? Good. Tell him it's Percy Cole. Thanks, I'll wait."

She sat back down, put her feet up on the desk, continuing to fan herself with her hat. Her wait was long, nearly five minutes, and just when she was beginning to wonder if the dispatcher forgot about her, she heard the voice of her father's long-time partner.

"Saints be preserved. Is this you, Percy?"

"It is, Mick."

"Sorry to keep you waiting but we was running a line-up. Pickpockets are rampant on Times Square, especially with sailors and soldiers on leave and drinking too much. What can I do for you, sweetheart? Everything all right with the family? That mischievous father of yours behaving himself?" His Irish brogue was thicker than ever now, but the joviality and friendship in his voice was still the same.

"Everything's fine, Mick, but I have a favor to ask of you."

"Ask away, darling. If it's mine to give, it's yours."

"I understand you are in charge of the investigation of the actor who died at the Royal Theatre, a Mr. Rutherford Carlisle.

"Yes." His voice was a little wary now. "That I am. What's it got to do with you?"

She stopped fanning her face and dropped her legs to the ground. What she said now mattered, if she was to get any help.

"Cole Investigations has been hired by Dexter Wainwright to find out what's going on behind some other mishaps around here during their production of..." she thought for a moment. "...the Scottish play. Something about a curse. It's a good job, Mick, even if it's only for a few days." She stressed the word job and avoided saying her part in it.

"So that fancy pants producer hired your father to go behind our backs and..." He cut himself off. "I knew I should have shut him down when I had the chance. Now La Guardia is in on it and wants to keep the show open for 'general good will'. Seems him and fancy pants are pals. But I'm still in charge here, and I won't be brooking no interference, even from Pop Cole." His voice was harsh and edgy.

Percy did some fast thinking. "Even if we can help you out? I'm on the scene. I've been hired as their assistant stage manager." The lie came out of nowhere and she went with it.

"What's that you say? They hired you to work there? I thought you said your father was snooping around--"

"Just on the curse thing, superstition stuff, mostly for Halloween."

"Halloween? What's that got to do with anything?"

"Publicity. They get to say they hired a private investigator to look into the curse hanging over this production of Macbeth. All those gory witches. Sells tickets."

"Oh, it does, does it?"

I'm winning him over.

"Sure." Her answer was glib. "And remember, one hand washes the other, Mick. These people will tell me a lot more than they would the cops. You know that."

The other end of the line went silent, but she could feel him thinking. As tempted as Percy was to press her point, she said no more, letting him stew over it.

"It would have to be unofficial," he finally said. "And you would have to tell me every time one of those characters passed gas."

There's an image I can live without.

"I'll be your very own private stool pigeon. But I'm going to have to know a few things, myself. What you found at the murder scene, stuff like that."

"Tell you what, you bring me a pastrami on rye, I'll give you a few tips, just so you or your father don't run aground. Where is Pop? Can I talk to him?"

More fast thinking. "Ah, no, he's winding up another case. I should be seeing him soon, though. I'll tell him I spoke to you."

"Ummm," O'Malley grunted. "You tell that son of a sidewinder to mind his P's and Q's while he's nosing around in this. I don't broo--"

"Yeah, yeah, I know. You don't brook no interference. I'll see you at noon. You want slaw with that?"

"Sauerkraut," he said, and hung up.

Chapter Six

Evelyn, I can't believe you killed him. What have we come to? Now I'm afraid. Not only were the police here, but I heard a rumor Wainwright has brought in a detective. It's only a woman, though. We can still be safe, but please don't take any more chances. Elsie.

P.S. I found Mamma's pearls packed away in a cardboard box. We could sell them and go back to England. Please!

Elsie

Chapter Seven

Percy glanced at her watch and remembered she'd forgotten to wind it. She ripped it off her wrist, and put the piece to her ear. Still ticking. As she wound the stupid thing, she noticed it was just past ten-thirty a.m.

Good. If my luck holds, maybe I can visit one of the people who took a powder, if they're still hanging around the City. Then get the pastrami on rye for O'Malley. And one for me, too.

Pop saved Mick's life in the line of duty. That was before the depression hit and most of the force got laid off, including Pop and Uncle Gil. Mick got lucky, with only six-month's seniority over the two Cole Brothers, who were the last to go.

A tentative knock on the door brought Percy back from the past. "Yeah." She hollered in the direction of the door. "Come on in."

Mavis stuck her head in, dark glossy curls in her medium bob bouncing. She smiled at Percy, but did not enter. "You sure it's okay?"

"Sure, I said come in. I meant come in."

That's an eight buck haircut if I've ever seen one. The dress ain't no piker, either.

"I've got that list for you, Miss Cole." She walked inside carrying her clipboard, offering the eight by eleven white sheet of paper. "Can I do anything else?"

Percy took the list and read it before answering. "Thanks. So the three items the cops took were a microphone, loudspeaker, and cord. I see this Dowell lives on Fifty-second and Seventh, and two more in Hell's kitchen. What's this one address unknown?" She looked up at Mavis, a puzzled expression on her face. "Don't you have to know everybody's address for tax purposes?"

"That would be Bert Asher; he was an extra. As a rule, yes, we do. We have to send everyone a W-Two form or a Ten Ninety-nine at the end of the fiscal year. Bert was staying at a rooming house up on One-hundred and Tenth Street."

"Well, what about this rooming house? Don't you have the address of that?"

"I did, but it won't do you any good. They had a fire ten days ago. You must have seen the article in the paper. It burned to the ground. It took the houses on either side with it. Two elderly people were killed. Very sad."

Percy sat bolt upright. "Was this before or after Asher quit?"

"Let me think. It was around the same time, I think. Yes, it burned down the night before. The next day, he didn't show up for rehearsal or the performance, either. At first we thought he'd been hurt in the fire, but one of the musicians said he noticed him outside the Automat that morning. When Bert saw him, he ran. We haven't heard from Bert since. And we owe him two weeks salary."

"So he did a bunk. Very interesting. Any listing of relatives, people to call in an emergency?"

"Just one of the other extras, Roland Gephardt. They've been friends for years. But when I asked Roland, he said he hadn't heard from Bert and had no idea where he was. Vaudevillians are a different breed, Miss Cole. They often travel from one show to the next using just a post office box for forwarding mail, but we don't even have that for Bert."

"You sound like you know something about these people."

"Theatre's the same the world over, I guess."

"Where you from?"

"California."

"Ah! I thought your accent was a little different. Lots of oranges. How long have you been working for Wainwright?"

"Not quite a year. I came straight out of secretarial school and got this job."

"What are you, twenty-two? What did you do before?"

"Why, I was in school, Miss Cole, and I'm only twenty."

"Nearly the same age as my kid sister." Percy digested this. "Give me this Roland Gephardt's phone number and address, just in case."

"Of course." Mavis wrote down a name on a slip of paper. "Did you want me to leave the room while you make a call to Felicity for an appointment?"

"Naw, I'll just show up. Might be better that way." Percy plopped her hat back on her head and moved toward the door. She turned around to face the young secretary. "Oh, Mavis, tell your boss not to hire anyone else for that assistant manager's job. I'll be stepping into it for a while."

A stricken look crossed Mavis's lovely face. "You? The assistant manager? But I don't understand. Do you know anything about the backstage management of a show?"

"Listen, I've been running an office for seventeen years, I have an eight-year old son, and I'm a fast learner. How tough can it be?"

"I see," Mavis said gravely. "In that case, you need to be back for a one o'clock call, a half hour before the performers. I'll let Mr. Wainwright know and alert Kyle, the stage manager, of the new hire."

"Do that." Percy's voice was equally grave. "And remember, this is a good cover for me, hanging around backstage looking into things. I'm counting on you not to tell anyone who I am or what I really do, not even the stage manager, what's his name." Not waiting for an answer, she wheeled around and left, the door shutting behind her.

Chapter Eight

Being back out in the real world was a shock in more ways than one. The sharpness of the sun and blistering heat hit Percy straight on even when she walked on the shadier side of the streets. Blasts of hot air coming from subway vents or vehicular exhaust made her feel like she was standing in front of an open pizza oven. Small particles of grit smacked her in the face and bothered her eyes.

Damn strike. Oy! All this schmutz floating around, as Mrs. Goldberg would say. I'm going to take a bath the minute I get home, which sounds grand. Cool water.

Trying to avoid the hoards of servicemen standing in line at the entrance to the USO, she crossed the street back into the sun looking for Felicity Dowell's address. She came to a tall but modest pale yellow brick building, maybe thirty stories high. Surprised to find no doorman, she went to a chrome intercom near the glass double-door entrance. Below were four rows of buttons next to names and apartment numbers. Further surprised, she found the actress's name listed with the others. She remembered Felicity Dowell as a British transplant during the late twenties, early thirties who became a big star. She'd be in her forties by now, at least. Apparently no one was haranguing the actress any more like the old days.

Hmmm. That's right. Performers, they're sort of like athletes. Nobody wants you when you're old and grey.

She depressed the button and held it down for a second or two. After a moment, there was the noise of static and a recognizable, albeit tinny sounding female voice. "Yes?"

"I'm looking for Miss Felicity Dowell. Is she available?"

There was a slight hesitation. "Who is it?"

"My name is Persephone Cole and I'd like to speak with her in person."

"What about?" The voice was on its guard.

"Miss Dowell, I have a small bequest for you and I am required to give it to you in person."

"A what?"

"A bequest." Percy repeated the lie that came easily to her. "For you."

"Well, who's it from?"

"You know, I'd really rather not discuss this down here where just anybody can listen in. Can I come up or should I just go away?" Percy stopped talking and waited. If she was any judge of humanity, the combination of curiosity and greed should get her through the locked door. A few more seconds of silence and the door buzzed and she heard the click of the lock being released.

She pushed open one of the glass door and stepped into a musty smelling lobby filled with plastic greenery and one or two dentist-style waiting room chairs. In front of her was an unmanned elevator, door open, waiting for a customer. She'd heard about these new-fangled elevators, as Pop called them, but had never ridden in one. Percy stepped inside, hoped the box would take her where she wanted to go, and pressed the twenty-seventh floor button. She had little concern about the fib she'd told.

I'll deal with it later. Before I leave, I'll get something out of her. I always do.

Percy exited the elevator and followed the numbers. Waiting at the end of a long hallway stood a woman wearing a grey and black bias-cut pants suit, her shoulders covered with a multi-colored scarf. Dyed black hair was artistically piled on top of her head.

Percy sized up the woman as she walked toward her. The actress leaned against the door jamb, swirling a glass of amber liquid and ice in her hand. The clinking sound of the cubes against the glass had a steady rhythm to them, sounding cool to Percy. The closer she got, the more she saw the beautiful face was covered by artfully applied makeup, not quite masking that she was a woman of a 'certain age'. The actress stared at Percy suspiciously then turned and called out to someone inside the apartment.

"Derek, Derek, darling. Come here, please."

A man in his late thirties came to the door. He was dressed in loose white trousers, wearing only an undershirt on top. A towel was thrown over a well-developed and muscular neck and shoulders. His muscles rippled as he watched Percy walk down the hall and toward
them. Even his ripples had ripples. He flexed his hands and arms repeatedly, his jaw grinding in unison.

I get it, buster. You're a strongman and if you have to, you'll take me down. Got it.

"How'd you know it was me? On the intercom?" Felicity Dowell said not quite guarding her doorway but not moving from it either.

"I'd know your voice anywhere, Miss Dowell. I've been listening to it on the radio for years. The RCA Drama Hour, wasn't it? And then Westinghouse Presents. You've been on a lot of those shows. You're a household name...and voice."

Okay, laying it on a little thick but these theatre types seem to like it.

Sure enough, Felicity Dowell broke out into a smile, and stepped to the side allowing Percy to enter her apartment. The strongman didn't budge.

"It's all right, darling. Let her in." She turned to Percy. "This is Derek. He takes care of me."

In more ways than one, I'll bet. Percy gave him a nod. Wordless, he turned on his heels and retreated behind a curtain into another room.

Once inside, Percy could see it was the apartment of a person who had seen better times but wasn't seeing them now. Large pieces of ornate furniture, in the style of Louie the Sixteenth, were crammed into a room far too small for them. The furniture was of a higher quality than the ones Percy had to contend with in her family's apartment, but it was still a lot of fake gilding, fancy stenciling, and clearly not the real thing.

When the king said, 'Apres moi, le deluge' or after me, the deluge, he probably hadn't meant a flood of horrible, imitation furniture. But that's so often the way. You get remembered for something that sends you spinning in your grave. Go figure.

As if reading her thoughts, the actress said, "You'll have to forgive the rooms. This is not my style. I'm post-modernist, myself.
I'm borrowing the apartment from a friend of mine who's on the west coast making a movie with Orson Wells. Not a very large part, but significant in demeanor. That's all we can hope for these days, parts of significance," she said, lowering herself into a throne-like chair and posing significantly.

Percy looked around. Walls, tabletops and counters anywhere there was free space was covered with photos and memorabilia of the once famous actress, touting her glorious and glamorous life.

"Impressive, aren't I?" Miss Dowell took a long drink of the liquid. "Don't let the press clippings fool you. I still put my makeup on one eyebrow at a time. May I offer you some refreshment? And before you get any ideas, this is iced tea. I haven't had a drink in three years, despite what Louella Parsons says. Sit down anywhere and tell me about the bequest." The woman threw her an ingenuous and disarming smile.

Percy remained standing. She was torn. She liked this woman and despite her best efforts, she *was* impressed.

This isn't going at all like I expected, and when you don't know what the hell to say, shoot for the truth.

"I have a confession to make, Miss Dowell."

"Oh?" Well plucked eyebrows shot up. She glanced in the direction of the departed Derek, as if anxious to summon him again should the need arrive.

"I don't have a bequest. I just said that to get in, to see you. I'm a private detective hired by Dexter Wainwright to look into the Macbeth curse. Apologies and all that, Miss Dowell, but I'd still like to ask you a few questions about what's been going on around there."

The regal pose gone, the actress stared at her for a brief time then burst into laughter.

"A lady detective? My goodness. Now we've all read Agatha Christie, but I thought lady detectives, if there truly is such a thing, were supposed to look like Miss Marple."

"You mean about a hundred years old, white-haired, and wearing a hand-crocheted pink shawl?" Percy grinned at Felicity Dowell. "I left my shawl at home."

"What color is your hair underneath that man's hat?" Percy removed the hat, allowing long, tangled red curls to fall, covering her neck and shoulders. "Ah! A glorious, flaming red. Hair the color
of which many an actress has ruined her own trying to attain. And then it never looks quite natural, as does yours. My hair color was a glorious raven black, but now it requires attention to keep it that way. Can you tell?" The actress ran ring-covered fingers through the darken hair. She looked at Percy's dubious face. "Never mind. They
haven't perfected the black color any more than the red. So you want to know why I left the production when it was supposed to have been a comeback for me?"

"I didn't know it was a comeback, Miss Dowell, but that makes your leaving all the more interesting. And I'd love some iced tea."

"Derek darling." The actress called out to the man in the next room. "Be a sweetie and bring Miss...Cole, is it?" Percy nodded. "Bring Miss Cole a glass of tea. Lots of ice." There was a muffled reply. "Thank you, sweetie." The actress looked at Percy and whispered. "He's a little on the simple side but quite appealing. And he'd lay down his life for me. With everything that's been going on, I need that."

"What exactly has been going on, Miss Dowell?"

The woman took a sip of her tea before replying. "It didn't start until we came to America. Frankly, I've done Lady Macbeth several times before and never had any trouble." She paused for a moment, reflecting on something in the past.

Derek entered the room carrying a small glass of iced tea, the sound of ice cubes tinkling within with each step he took. It was a lovely sound. He thrust the glass in Percy's outstretched hand.

"Thanks."

Again, without saying anything, Derek turned on his heels and left. "Not much of a talker," Percy remarked.

"No, but he does other things so very well." A slight smile splayed across her face. It hardened, as she changed subjects. "About Macbeth, I *am* reminded of one time on the London stage, back in nineteen-thirty. We had a rash of bad luck. One or two of my fellow actors were involved in accidents, nothing fatal, and part of the scenery caught fire and burned. The theatre closed down for three days. I'm glad nothing fatal has happened on this production, but I had a close call with that lorry."

Apparently, she hasn't heard about Carlisle yet. Sure, it happened too late to make the morning papers. It'll be out this afternoon. I'll keep a lid on it for now. It'll just rattle her.

"Lorry," Percy said aloud. "That's British for truck, right?"

"Yes, sorry. He came out of nowhere and headed right for me. It was ghastly. I had to throw myself on the sidewalk.

Ruined my silk stockings. I don't have to tell you how hard those are to come by these days."

"You said 'he'. Did you get a good look at him?"

"You mean, while I was flying through the air? As a matter of fact, I saw his face through the windshield or rather, the beard, that odious beard. It was hideous."

"Beard? What color?"

"A long, scruffy black thing. Frightening. Covered over half his face. I don't remember anything but that beard. I have nightmares over it."

"Is that when you decided to quit the show?"

"No, not even that would have driven me away from a part like Lady Macbeth. It was the letter."

"What did it say?"

"I've got it somewhere here, if you'd care to see it."

"Yeah, I would."

"Derek,' she called out again. "Would you be a love and get that letter to show Miss Cole? He's such a dear." She turned to Percy.

Derek entered the room instantly, as if he'd been standing on the other side of the door waiting to be summoned. He crossed to a small secretarial desk, opened one of the drawers and pulled out a folded sheet of paper. He crossed the room to Percy, handed her the paper and left the room again.

Percy unfolded the creased and tattered paper. The first thing she noticed was the different sized, cut out letters used to form words, and pasted on the page. Some were underlined for emphasis, others were in capital letters.

Leave the show or you will die. This is your only warning. The next time, I will not miss. Forever.

"You got the envelope this came in?"

"No I threw it away. I threw the letter away, as well, but Derek rescued it from the trash can."

"Have you shown it to the police?"

"No, I haven't." She hesitated.

"Why not?"

"I...I..."

"You're stuttering."

"I...showed it to Dexter and he told me he'd let me out of my contract if I didn't take it to the police."

"I see." Percy's eyes narrowed on the still beautiful actress. "Why do you think he did that?"

"I have no idea, and I don't care." She paused and took a deep breath. "It might have something to do with Macbeth. Or the musical I did before it, Stars and Stripes Forever."

"You mean, because of the word 'forever' at the end of this note?"

Felicity Dowell nodded, biting her lower lip. "You should talk to Dexter about this, but it was right around the time there was that trouble with his partner's death. I didn't follow it all, but Dexter did his usual raping of the innocent souls routine, I'm sure."

"Stars and Stripes Forever." Percy mused. "Wasn't that an American musical revue? I thought you were a classical trained, English actress."

Miss Dowell let out a throaty laugh. "When you're at the end of your career, it's the same as starting out. You'll do almost anything. And I can do an American accent, sing a little, and I've always been a dancer. Dexter thought I'd give the production a little class. As I was between engagements, so to speak, I opened the show on London's West End for a twelve-month contract."

"Did you ever meet his partner?"

"No, he died before the play went into production. I heard about him and that he died, but other than that, I don't know anything." The actress gestured with beautifully manicured hands.

Percy looked down at her own hands.

Oy!

"There was also something about you being poisoned, Miss Dowell. When did that happen?"

"I wasn't off the boat for twenty-four hours when I drank some bad tea. I know it was the tea. It tasted so funny."

"Where did you get the tea? Hope this isn't it." Percy pointed to the glass in her hand.

The actress laughed softly. "No, this is Earl Gray. I don't know where that other tea came from. They usually keep some around the theatre, I believe. We Brits like our tea. I had my dresser bring a cup to my dressing room in between shows. I only took a sip, but within minutes I felt dizzy and weak. It was terrible."

"Who or what is a dresser? Sounds like a piece of furniture."

"That's the person who helps you in and out of your costumes during the performance. They're part of the wardrobe union. There's a wardrobe supervisor, her assistant and then the
dressers. Everyone has one, although the lesser roles share, sometimes one dresser to six or seven actors. My dresser or I should say my ex-dresser is working with Cynthia now. Cynthia was my understudy and moved right into the part, within minutes of my leaving, I might add. She's a little young for the role, but you have to take your opportunities where you can in this business."

Percy put the empty glass down and stood. "Pretty much the same in my line of work. One more thing, mind if I keep this?" She folded the threatening letter and put it in her pocket, without waiting for the other woman's consent. "It might prove useful somewhere along the line."

Felicity Dowell shrugged and rose from the chair. "Whatever you'd like. I'm out of it now. In three days time I'm heading back to England to begin rehearsals for Medea. Lawrence Olivier will be directing."

"When did you negotiate that?"

The woman looked stunned. She brought her hand up to her throat and forced a smile. "I…I...don't understand."

"These parts that actors do, especially when they're at your level, aren't there agents and people like that involved? Doesn't it take weeks, if not months of negotiating? How is it you're going into another role in such a short amount of time?"

An embarrassed chirp rose from the actress's throat. "I...well…Larry and I have been talking about it for some time, having these 'if only I was free' conversations. Medea is a role to kill for. So when I was free, I wired him immediately and he wired back, offering me the role. It was most fortuitous."

"That's one word for it." Percy allowed a smile to cross her face. "Thanks for talking to me, Miss Dowell and sorry about the little white lie. Be sure to thank Derek for the iced tea." Percy crossed the room and opened the door, thinking.

Medea killed both her kids to get back at the king. Did Felicity Dowell kill anybody to play her life story? We'll see.

She glanced back to see a nervous or maybe guilty actress staring after her. Percy closed the door behind her.

Chapter Nine

Elsie, don't be angry. I had to do it. Carlisle followed me up to the catwalk and found me cutting one of the ropes. He threatened to go to Wainwright and tell him. Then he lunged at me. I tried to defend myself, pushed him away, but he lost his balance and went over. I was afraid someone might have heard his screams as he fell, but I think everyone was gone. I left the microphone and the cord where I found them. I know the police took them, but their existence might be to our advantage. I don't trust this woman detective, but if she gets in our way, we will deal with her. I don't trust any of them. They have no idea what wrong has been done us, but Wainwright does and he will pay. They will all pay.

P.S. Keep the pearls. Mamma would have wanted you to have them.

Evelyn

Chapter Ten

Roland Gephardt's address was a third-floor walk up about six blocks and several light years away from Felicity Dowell's place. At Eleventh Avenue and Forty-Seventh Street, this section of Hell's Kitchen was seedier than most. It was life lived amidst squalor in run-down buildings that nobody cared much about, including city officials. Percy stepped over a derelict lying on the front stoop, either high on something or sleeping it off. She decided not to ask which.

The lock was missing from the partially opened front door. Percy noticed it rusting in a corner of the filthy hallway. Pried open mailboxes, now twisted, useless metal, hung on a wall. By the looks of it, the same tool was used on them that broke the lock. None of it had been done recently. Roland Gephardt was the only name she could see anywhere, so she hiked up to the third floor where it said he lived.

Next to this place, she thought as she climbed the stairs, *I live in a palace. There's a sobering thought for a gal from the lower east side. But still. This man works on Broadway. What the hell does he do with his money?* Percy knocked on the door, angling to find out.

"You Roland Gephardt?"

She studied the face of the unshaven man closing in on sixty years of age. He'd opened the door wearing a tattered bathrobe haphazardly tied at the waist, revealing a chest of matted grey hair. "Sorry to have awakened you."

He yawned in her face. "Who wants to know?" He leaned against the door, less than half way open. "Who are you?"

"Dexter Wainwright sent me."

At the sound of the producer's name, Gephardt straightened up and wiped the sleep from his eyes and mouth. "Mr. Wainwright sent you? Why? Am I being fired or something?"

"Why would you think that? Can I come in?" She pushed at the door. Thrown off-balance, he stepped aside, allowing her entrance into the apartment.

It was a small, cluttered room, smelling of dirty clothes and cigarette smoke. An unmade bed, only two or three feet from the door, had an empty bottle of vodka lying at its foot. Gephardt saw that she saw the bottle and made a grab for it. In his haste, the belt to his robe came undone, revealing baggy and faded boxer shorts.

"You better tie yourself up. In case you're on the shy side." She watched him scramble to find a place for the empty bottle and close his robe. "Then you're going to tell me why you thought I was here to fire you."

"I don't understand. If he didn't send you to fire me, what do you want? I don't have to be at the theatre for another two hours."

"I want an answer to what I just asked. Why do you think I came here to fire you?"

Gephardt walked over to a dresser littered with old newspapers, ashtrays loaded with cigarette butts, and empty glasses. He pushed through the mess in search of an unsmoked cigarette before he spoke. Finding one, he lit it and turned to Percy.

"With everything that's been going on around that theatre, it wouldn't surprise me if we all got canned. I never seen a play so cursed."

"Like what happened to your friend, Bert Asher?"

"Oh, Bert," Gephardt said, taking a deep drag from the cigarette and exhaling it slowly in Percy's face. It took him a moment to realize what he was doing. "Sorry. I was trying to think."

"Sometimes that's not as easy as it sounds."

"Yes." He nodded then looked at her, unsure of whether or not he'd been insulted. He clamped down on the end of the cigarette and chewed it between browning teeth.

"Bert and me, we go way back," he finally said. "Vaudeville, Bert and me. We were hoofers back then in the chorus. But those days are over. The circuit's pretty much gone now and we're too old. Being a spear carrier is all that's left, when you can get it. Thirteen-fifty a week, and we're lucky to get that. Can you imagine?" He shook his head and crossed over to a small chair in the corner of the room, throwing himself into it.

"Tell me about Bert and his rooming house burning down."

He glared at her over the hazy smoke drifting up from his cigarette. "What did you say your name was?"

"I didn't, but it's Percy Cole. I'm the new assistant stage manager and my job is to make sure the cast and crew is happy in their job."

"What?"

"Bert wasn't happy." She removed her hat and fanned herself with it. "And I want to know why. Just to make sure the rest of the cast stays happy and doesn't take it on the lam like good, old Bert. Hot in here, isn't it?"

"Yeah, it is. I had a fan but it stopped working."

"Why don't you open a window?"

"I don't want those pigeons flying in. When I open the windows, that's what they do. Damn birds." He crossed one leg over the other and studied her for a moment. His robe fell open. He didn't notice or care. "You say part of your job is going around and finding out if we're happy or not? I never heard of such a thing."

"You have to admit, Mr. Gephardt, some pretty extraordinary things have been going on around this production of Macbeth."

He started at hearing the name of the play said out loud, his crossed leg pulling off the other one and coming down with a thud. He leaned forward, a worried expression crossing his face.

"Don't be saying that name out loud, even outside the theatre. Bad enough things have been happening without doing that."

"Like?"

"Like that fire you mentioned. It started in Bert's room, you know. He told me. He said he woke up in time to see somebody crawling out the window and onto the fire escape."

"A man, a woman, what?" Percy was quick to ask. "What did the person look like?"

"He didn't say. Maybe he was too busy screaming and getting out of there. There was a fire in the corner of his room, he said, a blaze, and it took off before he could do anything. He just ran out the door and yelled 'fire'. Then everybody got out of that dried up old place."

"Two people didn't make it, I understand," Percy said, quietly.

"That wasn't Bert's fault. If he hadn't yelled like he did, a lot of others would have been caught in it. Bert said the fire took off like

it had gasoline in it or something. He was lucky to get out alive, he said."

"Did he tell the police what he saw?"

"Bert? He doesn't talk to police. He did time upstate for writing bad checks. He doesn't talk to police," Gephardt repeated.

"So they don't know about the person in his room."

The man shrugged. "Guess not. I didn't tell anybody what he said to me. Except you."

"Where is Bert? Where did he go?"

Gephardt shrugged again and stubbed his cigarette out in an already overflowing ashtray on a small table by his chair.

"Mr. Gephardt, you're a smart man."

No you're not, but sometimes a fib will get me some place, so I'm going with this one.

"Smart enough to keep my mouth shut," he replied, with a smirk.

"Aw, but sometimes that's not so smart. Mr. Wainwright would be very grateful to someone who cooperated with him in getting to the bottom of this. Might be worth, say, fifteen-fifty a week from now on."

"You can do that? You can increase my salary like that?"

Percy hedged her bets a little. "Well, maybe. I can try. As I said, he would be grateful."

Gephardt let out a bark of a laugh. "You don't know Wainwright much, do you? He don't get grateful like that. Too cheap. I did another show with him right before this one."

"You mean, Stars and Stripes Forever?"

"Sure. I told you I was a hoofer. I did some dancing in the background, filled in the crowd scenes. Cheap bastard only paid me fourteen bucks a week for that. And with me dancing two numbers, too. Sorry I don't have any place for you to sit down," he said, suddenly overcome with gentlemanliness. "Only the one chair." He gave her an apologetic smile.

"Don't worry about it. Bert work Forever with you?"

"We were both in the chorus. We even did part of our old Vaudeville routine together. Didn't get paid any more, but we did it anyway."

"Trip down memory lane?"

"Something like that."

"Anything happen on that show? Something that stands out in your mind?"

"No, not a thing. Wait a minute. I remember reading the wife of Wainwright's partner died in England about a year after his partner did, but that's about it." Roland reflected for a moment. "Yeah, that's right. Cohen died before the musical went into production and the wife died while we were in performance. There was even an article about it in Variety, saying Stars and Stripes Forever was jinxed. We thought Wainwright was going to say something at one of the shows, you know, like a tribute."

"Did you know Jacob Cohen?"

"Yeah, I done a couple of shows for the two of them before the older one, Cohen, up and died. Uppity old geezer, thought he was better than everybody. They'd been partners for a long time. You think he would have said something, that's all. But that's Wainwright. That's why I'm surprised he sent you on to see me like this. I didn't think he gave a tinker's damn."

"So do you know where Bert might be? We'd like to send him his last paycheck."

"Why don't you give it to me? I'll see that he gets it."

Percy shot him an incredulous look.

"Hey, Bert's the one who did time for forging checks, not me," Gephardt said, defensively.

"Where is he, Gephardt? Tell me."

He got up and went to the dresser in search of another cigarette. "Jesus Christ, I'm out of fags." He brushed at the top of the dresser, sending ashy butts flying through the air.

"I'll buy you a carton of those things, if you'll tell me what I want to know."

His face brightened as he turned to her. "Oh, what the hell. I'm not even sure that's where he is, but I'll tell you, anyway. He's got a wife, an ex-wife, out in Phoenix. It's a hot hellhole like this, but all the time, all year long. He says she's got emphysema or some such thing and has to be there for her health. He goes out and stays with her from time to time. I think he's there now. At least, that's where he was heading. She still goes by his name. Mrs. Bert Asher," he said, rolling the name around in his mouth. "Like it meant something to be married to him. You really going to mail him his last pay? He could use it."

"I am. I'll see that he gets it." She reached into her pocket and drew out two folded dollar bills. "By the way, do you know if he got any threatening letters right before he left?"

"Sure, we all did." Gephardt reached for the cash but Percy pulled her hand back.

"Who's 'we all'?"

"All six of us in the dressing room."

"Did you tell anyone about it?"

"Naw, we thought it was funny, over the top, you know?" He laughed at the memory then began to cough. It took him a moment to get the coughing under control. Percy waited.

"We figured it was Sir Anthony," he went on. "He was always doing something like that, playing up the witches' curse. His idea of a joke, but Bert took it hard. Went and complained about it, for all the good something like that does you."

"Did he?" Percy mused for a moment. "Know who he talked to?"

"What am I, his mother? He's just like that. A mousy kind of guy. Takes everything serious. Good friend, though," Gephardt added wistfully. "I miss him."

Percy watched a look akin to sorrow cross the man's face. "Gephardt, what the hell are you doing in a dump like this? It seems to me you could do better, even at the occasional thirteen-fifty a week."

"I own the place," Gephardt said with a straight face.

"Excuse me?"

'Yeah, I bought it twenty, twenty-five years ago. It's a place to flop when I'm in town. Nobody else lives in the building. I got it to myself."

"I'll bet," she said, as she handed him the money. "Here you go. One thing, though, sort of as a warning..." She broke off speaking and looked into his eyes.

Gephardt took the money but stared back at her questioningly.

"I'd put a working lock on that downstairs door." She turned and moved to leave. "You never know when someone's going to creep up those stairs in the middle of the night and kill you."

"Vaudeville already did that, lady," she heard Gephardt call after her, as she closed the door behind her.

Chapter Eleven

"Yeah," said Percy to the older, balding man behind the counter of the Carnegie Deli. "That's three pastramis on rye, two with slaw, the other with kraut, pickles on the side. Throw in a celery soda and two cream sodas. Give me an extra bag, while you're at it. This is to go."

She'd been standing in line for nearly twenty minutes. This was one of the few places in Manhattan that rarely ran out of meat, so the short hike up to Fifty-fifth Street was worth it.

Whenever Percy was in mid-town, the Carnegie Deli called to her louder than the mythical sirens, despite the lousy service. Besides, she knew O'Malley. Nothing softened him up more than a good pastrami on rye. Or Pop. If things worked out the way she wanted, she'd hand one of these to him in person. If not, she'd bring the extra sandwich home to him as a peace offering. That is, if she didn't eat it herself beforehand.

"You got a payphone around here? Hey!" She banged on the countertop, when he didn't respond. "I said, you got a payphone around here?"

The man, whose only words to her had been 'Whaddaya want?' glanced up from his order pad to give Percy a look of distain. He slapped the receipt on the glass top of the high counter.

"You're number seventy-three. Pay by the door. Behind you in the corner over there," he said without a smile, gesturing to the dark wood phone booth freestanding near the fire exit.

She squeezed her large frame in between dozens of people crammed around small tables piled high with food. Everyone was eating, laughing, and talking at the top of their lungs, military and civilians alike. If it hadn't been for the uniformed men, it was almost as if the war didn't exist.

And all this noise adds to the charm.

The phone booth was empty and Percy sidled in, closing the door behind her. The thick door blocked out most of the din, offering relative quiet. Percy removed two nickels from her pocket and inserted one in the coin slot, anxious to talk to her son.

"Murray Hill four-seven-seven-three," she muttered then dialed. After three rings, the phone was answered by a woman.

"Hello?"

"Sylvia? Percy Cole here. How are you?"

"I'm fine, Percy, just fine. Do you want to talk to Oliver? He's right here. The boys are designing their Halloween costumes," she added. "Oliver's a good artist. You can tell his is the Green Lantern. Freddy says he wants to be Superman, but it looks more like a blue blob."

She let out a light laugh. Percy did, too, but there was something in the other woman's laugh that caused Percy concern. "Sylvia, are you all right?"

"I'm fine, fine." Her answer came a little too bright and cheery. After a moment's silence, Sylvia lowered her voice. "I haven't had a letter from Fred in over a week. I'm a little…scared, that's all. I'm sure I'll get one tomorrow. But you know, he writes every other day."

"They would have notified you by now, Sylvia, if anything was wrong. It's probably a hang-up with the post office. You know how they are. They'd misplace a building if you could shove it in an envelope for them."

Sylvia's laugh was genuine now. "Maybe you're right. Hang on a minute, let me get Oliver."

Percy heard the sound of the phone being set down. She'd been flippant about the post office. The mail came from the Army, anyway, and they tended not to make mistakes.

Jeesh, this is the down side of having a husband you care about. With Leo the Louse, I only hope wherever he is, he never sends me a letter.

"Hello, Mommy?"

The sound of Oliver's small voice warmed her all over. This was the child who gave her life meaning.

"Hello, sweetie."

"Mommy," he burst out. "Somebody stole our jack-o'-lantern, right from our front door! And they took Freddy's, too. And

Mrs. Rendell says they took the neighbors, too. Somebody's stealing our pumpkins!"

"Someone took our jack-o'-lantern?" Guilt rushed through her. She'd been so eager to leave the apartment and get to the new job, she hadn't even noticed the pumpkin's absence. "When did you see it was missing? This morning?"

"No ma'am. It was there when I left. Grandma called and asked if I took it with me to cub scouts, but I didn't. Gee, Mommy," he whined, "I worked real hard on that pumpkin. I even gave him a crooked smile and everything."

"Well, don't you worry about it, Oliver." Her answer was a little too bright, even to her ears. "I'll get another one, a larger one, and we'll carve it all over again. This time it'll be even better. Practice makes perfect."

"Okay. Can I put a candle in it?"

"We'll see. Tell me what you've been doing today, sweetie."

"I made five teepees out of popsicle sticks. One for you, one for Grandpop, one for grandma, one for Aunt Sera and one for me. They look like teepees, too!"

His enthusiasm was catching. "I'll bet they do. I can't wait to see mine. Are you having fun?"

"Yes ma'am. Freddy asked if I can stay for dinner. Can I, Mommy, can I? They're having hotdogs and beans!"

"Well, if it isn't too much trouble for Mrs. Rendell."

"It's not. She says I have very grownup manners."

"I'm glad to hear it. If you promise to take your dish to the sink afterward, you can stay."

"Yah!"

"Listen, sweetie, Mommy has to work tonight, so let's go to the movies tomorrow afternoon instead of tonight, okay?"

"Okay, Mommy. Can I listen to the Green Lantern tonight?"

"I don't think so, sweetheart. That's kind of late and you're already having a pretty full day. You wash up and go to bed right away when you get home."

"Awwww," he grumbled.

"Awwww, yourself. We can't have everything in this life. When you get finished eating, it'll be dark, so I'm going to ask Mrs.
Rendell to walk you down to the curb and watch you cross the street to the apartment. You do everything she says, okay?"

"Okay, Mommy."

"Put Mrs. Rendell back on the line. I love you, sweetie."

"I love you, too, Mommy."

After working the logistics of getting her son back home, Percy hung up. She dialed the other number thinking of a plan to deal with her father, hoping it would do the trick. He was somewhat more difficult than Oliver to get to do what she wanted. But not impossible.

A young female voice answered the phone on the fifth ring.

"Hello?"

"Hi, Sera. Pop up or is he still sleeping?"

"Oooooooo, you are in so much trouble!" Sera's voice had a gleeful, sing-song quality to it. "When Mother told Pop where you went and what you were up to, he hit the roof."

So much for Mother keeping a secret.

"He's going to kill you," Sera went on.

"Try not to sound so happy."

"Better you than me. Wish I could be around when you two go at it, but I'm going to the movies. I'm seeing a John Wayne double feature. What a dreamboat. Did you know his real name is Marion Morrison?"

"I did."

"I read that in a magazine. We're not the only family with screwball names. Did you take the carved pumpkin from in front of the door and throw it away or something?"

"Why on earth would I do that, Sera? Oliver and I spent hours carving that thing."

"And it still looked like someone went at it with a meat cleaver."

"Just keep your remarks to yourself and put Pop on the line. May as well get it over with," Percy muttered.

"Pop!" Sera screamed into the mouthpiece.

"Ow. Give a body a warning where you're going to do that, Sera."

There was no reply, but rather the shuffle of a phone and then a clunk. After a few seconds she heard Pop's indignant voice.

"Persephone Cole, what is the meaning of this?"

"Hi, Pop. Listen, can you chew me out later? I hope Ophelia's got enough gas to get you to midtown. Right now I need your help."

"She's got plenty of gas. I put three gallons in her just this morning. What do you mean, you need my help? Where are you? And this better be good."

"Pop, I know you're working nights, but --"

"Not any more. I just got canned. Rabbis' ran out of money. I'm going to keep at it on my own, though. There's some kids, Nazi sympathizers..." He sputtered for a minute. "Now you stop distracting me, young lady. What do you mean, taking a job as a detective? And for fifteen dollars a day! It better be honest."

"It's in the theatre, Pop, and with this lot, how honest it is, is questionable. However, I'm going undercover as the assistant stage manager, so I need you to be my feet while I'm doing whatever an assistant stage manager does. You have to have lunch with O'Malley and get the low-down on this Carlisle death --"

"O'Malley?" Pop interrupted. "Mick O'Malley? And who's Carlisle?"

"Mick's handling the case and he's looking forward to seeing you," she added as an embellishment. "The stiff in question, name of Carlisle, was an actor playing the part of Macduff. Fell to his death last night. I need some details, as only the cops can have. Then I need you to go the public library at Forty-second and Fifth and look up some people in 'Who's Who in the Theatre'. I'll give you a list of names when I see you. There's a Carnegie Deli pastrami on rye in it for you."

"Pastrami? On rye?" Percy could almost see Pop lick his lips. "And here Mother was making her milk fish stew tonight." His voice carried insincere regret.

Percy let out an involuntary shudder. Mother's milk fish stew consisted of fish heads cooked for hours in half water, half canned milk, with tons of onions, carrots and celery thrown in.

"That must be why Oliver was so insistent on eating with Freddy." Percy let out a hoot of laugher. "By the way, you want to let Mother know? Tell her he'll be home right after, around seven or seven-thirty."

"That leaves the milk fish stew for the stray dogs in the neighborhood."

"Even they won't touch it, Pop."

"Let's not tell Mother. Am I getting slaw and a cream soda with that pastrami?"

"Natch. I'll meet you outside the Royal Theatre at Forty-sixth and Broadway in twenty minutes."

"Make it fifteen."

Chapter Twelve

Elsie, you put the dagger back in place barely in time. I tried to warn you, but heard someone coming and hid behind some scenery until they left. I don't think they saw me or you, either, but we can't be too careful. I wish we could be together more often, but it's not possible. I'm sorry about the fire, but it couldn't be helped. Like us, there are many innocent victims in this world. We must steel our hearts to them.

Evelyn

Chapter Thirteen

Percy watched the backside of Ophelia disappear into midtown traffic. The black nineteen-twenty-nine Dodge was considered more of a family pet than the family car. It was old but reliable, except when you ran out of gas, which happened more often than not.

Percy turned from the street and went into the theatre, looking at her watch. Twelve-fifteen. Enough time for a little chat before she went to her new job.

"How you doing, Ned?" Percy leaned her face into his small space with a grin.

Ned looked up from the newspaper, watery eyes fastening on her. "Well, if it ain't our own private dick," he said with a smile.

"Shhhh. Mum's the word on that."

"Gotcha."

"Interested in sharing a pastrami on rye? Straight from the Carnegie."

"Don't mind if I do," he said, folding his newspaper and tucking it in the back pocket of his pants.

Percy opened the small bag, took out the thick, meaty sandwich neatly cut in half and began to unwrap the thin paper containing it. She looked around her. "Who's in the theatre?"

"Not many." He grabbed one of the halves. "It's lunchtime. I don't get relieved until around two-fifteen and then it's only for twenty minutes. I try to bring my lunch, but sometimes the missus forgets to make it. Today's one of those days," he added, taking a huge bite.

Percy followed suit, took a bite, and rolled her eyes. "Ambrosia," she murmured.

"Thought it was pastrami," Ned said with a full mouth, spraying specks of food here and there. "Tastes like it."

"Yeah." Percy dropped the sandwich on the paper and wrapped it up again.

Emily Post would not approve of Ned's table manners and as a mother, neither do I.

She wiped flecks of Ned's food from the sleeve of her suit before she spoke again. "So exactly who's here right now? And you can wait and tell me after you get through swallowing. Have some coleslaw." She pushed the small container forward and Ned grabbed it.

He gulped down his mouthful and wiped his maw on the sleeve of his well-worn plaid shirt. "Let's see." He thought for a moment, while he picked up a fork from one of the small cubicles and wiped it on his pants leg. "All them actors are gone. They had a 'brush up' rehearsal earlier. That's where they run lines or something. Big ta-do over that actor fellow falling to his death, but Wainwright said it was because he went up on the catwalk, which is dangerous. He said, let that be a warning. Nobody but someone who knows what they're doing should be up there."

"What was the reaction to that story?"

"You know how simple them show folk are. They believe what they want."

"Most people are like that," Percy remarked.

"True enough. All that was over about fifteen minutes ago and them actors stampeded out of here for lunch. Backstage crew ain't set to arrive for another twenty minutes or so. They got to be here an hour before the show; the actors half hour. This ain't no show today, but they're going to do a 'run-through'. You know what that is?"

"I do. Who else is inside right now?"

He crammed a forkful of coleslaw in his mouth then opened it to speak.

"Wait," said Percy. "Let me tell you. We'll make it a game, Ned. Wainwright, he here?" Ned nodded. "His secretary?" Ned nodded again and swallowed.

"Yup, she's here. So is the director, that swishy fellow, and the new stage manager, that kid who thinks he's too good for anybody, and of course, the hammy actor, *Sir* Anthony Slattery. He's always here. It's like he lives here."

"You say he's always here. Do you have to be here, too?"

"Not unless they tell me. He's got his own keys to the theatre. All them that are here now have their own keys."

"So they can come and go anytime they please. That's interesting." Ned eyed the pickle. "Take the pickle, Ned."

"You're sure?"

"I'm sure." He grabbed it and chomped down with enthusiasm.

"What was this Rutherford Carlisle like?" She picked up the celery soda, jammed the top into the doorframe, and pushed back. The cap snapped off with a popping sound, followed by carbon fizz. She took a slug while she listened to the old man.

"Oh, like them all, full of himself. He liked the ladies. Of course, he was married once to the first one who played the gal part, so everybody was friendly to him."

"Felicity Dowell?"

"Yup. She called him 'Rudy darling'. They was still friends, if you can imagine that. Divorced and all. You married?" He quizzed her out of the blue, narrowing his eyes on her.

"I was. Not anymore."

"You like to call that man 'darling'?

What I'd like to call that man is 'dead'.

"No, I don't," she said aloud. "But let's stick to this group. What interesting tidbits do you know about anybody else?"

"Want to get your three bucks worth?"

"And a half a sandwich."

"Fair enough." He laughed, his face turning red. "Well...everybody's been fooling around with everybody or trying to. Them's theatre folk for you."

"Like who?"

"Wainwright's been chasing after that secretary of his, even though he's got him a wife not much older. The director has taken up with one of them second bananas. Lennox, I think. But it's on the sly. You don't want something like that getting out. Normal folks don't like it."

"A second banana. That's a sidekick of the main star. Vaudeville, right?"

He nodded, now deep in thought. He ticked off people on the fingers of his hand. "Carlisle was having a time with one of them gals who plays a witch and some other part; Laverne's her name.

The new stage manager's girlfriend is the assistant wardrobe supervisor, Alice. They always got their heads together. Pretty little thing, but too good for everybody, just like him."

"That would be Kyle." Ned nodded again. "He's going to be my new boss for a time. What can you tell me about him?"

"Not one blessed thing. He keeps to himself. Only says 'good morning', things like that. The first stage manager, he used to bring me coffee, stuff to eat, like you done. It's always good to get along with the stage door attendant. I can keep people away he don't want to see. Or I can let them in, no matter what he says. If you're going to be working for him, you should tell him."

She tilted back the bottle and finished off her soda. "If I get a chance. Anything else? What about Sir Anthony?"

"Him," exclaimed Ned. "Bigger than life, that one. He plays practical jokes, likes to gamble and play cards. Thinks it's manly. Always roping the other actors into playing poker with him at all hours, especially after the show. Bets the nags; his bookie's been here often enough. He's a drinker, too, although never before a show."

"I've read that," Percy interjected.

"And he'll bed down anything that walks slow enough." Ned added more, as an afterthought. "Has an odd-looking cat. Takes it everywhere with him; devoted to it. Animal lover, I'll give him that."

"You're quite the philosopher, Ned."

The old man shrugged. "I been around. Anyways, he's taken up with that new filly, the one who's doing the gal lead now. She thinks it's going to get her somewhere." Ned let out a half-laugh, half-snort.

"The woman playing Lady Macbeth?"

"That's the one, only they don't like it when you say the name. I've learned not to. Cynthia Beauchamp. Pretends she's from the continent. She's from the Bronx; I knew her when."

"When what?"

"When she was Myrtle Bassett."

Percy let out a chuckle and picked up her uneaten sandwich. "Ned, it's been grand talking to you. I'm learning from a master," she said, turning to leave. She looked back over her shoulder. "Remember, keep who I am under your hat. All you know is, I'm the new assistant stage manager. Got it?"

"Won't get it out of me." He shook his head with pride. "I mind my own business."

Chapter Fourteen

Evelyn, I sent out another letter last night, just as you've asked. I'm glad you thought better about stopping them. Must I meet you tonight in that awful place? The climb is so horrible. Why can't we meet somewhere else? Tomorrow is my birthday. Can't we do something nice on my birthday? I would so love that.

Elsie

Chapter Fifteen

Percy strode past the producer's office into the backstage area, and toward the stage. She stopped in a five-foot wide path between two sets of dark burgundy velvet curtains hanging from the eighty-foot grid by ropes. Unwrapping her sandwich again and munching on it, Percy studied her surroundings. From attending her son's second grade production of Pinocchio, she knew this section of the stage was called the wings. Part of the stage deck, but out of sight of the audience, this was where performers entered and exited the play.

Inside each wing and also out of sightline, light poles stood ten to fifteen feet tall. Up the side of each pole starting from the middle to the top, a line of floodlights were attached by c-clamps. Lenses covered the lights in one of five colors, blue, red, yellow, pink, or white and each was aimed at a particular section of the stage. Layered sandbags were stacked on their wide bases, a measure of security against toppling over. Dark and unused for the moment, they stood like silent sentinels guarding the empty stage against further catastrophe.

Straight ahead was the stage, devoid of furniture or scenery and gloomy in its dimness. A lone, white light, covered with the same protective metal screening as the lights on the walls, sat thirty to thirty-five feet ahead at center stage on a four-foot stand. It cast long, strident shadows.

Out front, beyond what was referred to as the 'fourth wall', was the auditorium or house, lavish in its painted murals, crystal chandeliers, and red velvet and gold seats. Percy glanced into the house. Hundreds of empty seats stared back at her. The effect was eerie and lonely.

She studied the proscenium arch separating the house, where the audience sat, from onstage containing the main stage acting and backstage areas. With the ornate and imposing proscenium arch
being nearly forty feet in height, that meant the ceiling behind it had to be double in order to accommodate the backdrops or flies lowered and raised during a production.

That's a lot of feet, baby.

Percy tilted her head back and looked up into the shadowy vastness of the eighty-foot high ceiling called the grid. She allowed her eyes to adjust to the dark for all the good it did her. Thirty-five feet in the air the narrow catwalk ran the length of the stage and wings, the one from which Carlisle fell to his death. More bags of sand, used as counterweights for stored scenery, hung from ropes and dangled precariously above. Unable to be seen, they were nonetheless there, tied on to railings on both sides of the catwalk.

That must be where the sandbag came from that fell on the stage manager, too. How the hell do you get up there?

Taking her last bite, her eyes scanned the back and side walls of the theatre, searching for stairs or steps. On each side wall of the theatre, a series of iron rungs ran up the wall leading to the catwalk. She walked toward the closest one, brushing the crumbs off her hands, and cupped her hand around an iron rung.

Not exactly the stairway to heaven, but it seems to be the only way to get to the catwalk. I'll climb up when I can and see exactly what's what up there. But I'll have to have a strong cup of coffee first.

Percy wheeled around and headed back to the producer's office. She stepped onto what's referred to as the side stage, a larger, better lit area providing access to offices and dressing rooms. From what she'd been told, there were dressing rooms on the ground floor and the second floor, with the basement used primarily for costumes, props, hair and wigs.

"Miss Cole," called out a female voice.

Percy paused mid-step, her head whipping around to the sound of Mavis's voice. This side of the proscenium was where the stage manager stood to cue the show and prompt performers, aptly called the prompt corner. The secretary and the newly crowned stage manager, Kyle, came out from either side of the podium and moved toward her with a distinct purpose.

"Hold that thought, kids," Percy said, with a nod and a smile. Then she opened the door of the producer's office, slamming it closed behind her.

Wainwright, seated behind his desk, was jarred by the sound of the closing door during his telephone discussion. He gave her a dirty look but resumed his conversation. Percy stood for a split second eyeing him. Then she walked over, snatched the phone from his hand, and talked into the mouthpiece.

"He'll call you right back."

She replaced the receiver on its instrument and glared down at the seated Wainwright who'd been too shocked to move.

A dark fury covered the producer's features. He leapt up from his chair and put his face level with her face, shouting, "How dare you! How dare you come in here and do something like that. Just who do you think --"

"Shut up and sit down," Percy ordered.

Taken aback, the man nearly fell into his chair, eyes round in astonishment. Her voice quiet but commanding,

Percy first shook a finger in his face then leaned over the desk until they were almost nose to nose.

"Listen, you. I told you over the phone this morning, you had to tell me the truth, all of it. Later on in this office, I asked you if there was anything else and you gave me a stall. Twice I've told you to level with me and twice you haven't. Three times and you're out. I've got a good mind to throw this check for forty-five bucks in your face and leave. And maybe I'll punch you in the snoot on my way out, just for the hell of it. But whatever, I'm keeping the expense money you gave me, because I don't like being lied to. So this is your call. Are you going to tell me the truth or am I hitting the road?"

"I haven't lied --"

"Omission is a lie," she said, her volume overriding his.

They glared at each other for a moment but Wainwright was the first to break down.

"Very well, I'll tell you whatever you want to know. But I don't think..."

"That's the trouble with you, Wainwright," she interrupted. "You don't think. But you're paying me to do it for you, so at least cooperate. Let's start with the production before this one, Stars and Stripes Forever. You helped develop it, right?"

"I brought it to where it is today." Pride overtook his indignation. "Like I did with this one."

"Yeah, with people getting maimed, killed, or running for their lives. So tell me, you get a threatening letter?"

"How did you know?" Wainwright pulled out a three-way folded sheet of paper from his breast pocket and handed it to Percy. "This showed up this morning. I found it in a stack of mail. I got so thrown by it, I called you."

She opened it and saw the same kind of pasted on cut out words as Felicity Dowell's. Percy read the brief letter aloud. "*You're next. Remember. Forever*. Not poetry, but the message is loud and clear. You got the envelope it came in?" She looked up at Wainwright and waited.

He turned to a stack of mail and searched. The producer chose a ripped envelope and tossed it across the table to her. Percy picked it up and looked at the canceled stamp in the corner.

"Mailed at the Thirty-fourth Street post office. Who opens your mail?"

"I do or my secretary does. This morning, I did."

"'Remember. Forever'. Remember what?"

"How should I know?" His attitude was belligerent. Percy raised an eyebrow and his tone mellowed. "I'm not sure, not exactly. It's why I didn't mention it before."

"Mention it now."

He hesitated then smiled at her in a conspiratorial way. "Listen, I'm not always the most likable guy in the world."

"No kidding."

"The truth is, I'm a businessman, Miss Cole. My job is to make money, to challenge the director, to foresee--"

"Stop telling me the reasons why you're an S.O.B. and stick to this," Percy waved the letter in his face. "Why did somebody send this to you? Last chance and then I'm going home to some milk fish stew, which is preferable to your baloney."

"All right, all right. I had a business partner," he said, chewing on the flesh around his thumbnail. "Jacob Cohen, someone who started me in the business. The last thing we did together was work on mounting Stars and Stripes Forever. It took us three years to get it going. Smash hit, still running down the street to sold out crowds. Previously, we'd had some duds, momentous losses. We were on the edge of bankruptcy. Even before casting Forever, we
knew it was going to be a winner. But several months before it opened, Cohen up and died unexpectedly, and..." He stopped speaking.

"And," Percy encouraged.

"We had never signed a waiver to the partnership agreement on that particular project. You have to do that if you want something else done with your share." He went back to chewing on his thumbnail.

"How long had you been partners?"

"Thirteen years." Wainwright waved a long, pointy finger in her face, as he took a deep breath. "These agreements are complicated but we'd always been fair with one another. Like I say, we hadn't signed anything and I had done most of the brainwork. There are six road companies of Forever, plus the Broadway show, even with the war on, and because of me. I look back on it, Jacob wasn't holding up his end then and hadn't been for months. It's a pity but there you are." He stood up, stretched his long six foot four frame, and gave her an innocent look.

"So he dies and you take it all."

"It's called Right of Survivorship. If you don't want your partner to inherit his half, you have to put it in writing."

"Cohen have a family?" He didn't answer but nodded. "Did his wife contact you? Ask for her husband's share?"

"Yes. You see, his wife had actually come up with the idea for the show, a Brit's view of the Yanks celebrating July Fourth, done in song and dance. Brilliant idea. Of course, I developed it."

"Before he died, though, I'll bet Cohen *said* he wanted his share to go to her, even though he hadn't gotten around to writing it down."

"Something like that." He looked at her appraisingly. "You're pretty quick. Anyway,

It was sort of a verbal partnership we had with his wife. She came a few times to our meetings before we went into production, several months before her husband died. Scatty, bird-like thing, his wife. But, like you say, he never got around to putting it in writing before he died. So the show became mine, lock, stock and barrel."

"Let me get this straight, you went and cheated the bird-like widow of your dead business partner even though the show was her idea? You're a louse." Percy stopped for a moment and thought. "Were there kids?"

"Yes, two girls, I think. I can't remember their names. I never met them. He never brought them around and rarely spoke of them. Cohen and I didn't socialize. He was upper Manchester, I was a Yank. We were strictly business."

"You're still a louse."

"Hey, business is business and I've got a family, too, you know." Wainwright bristled. "Two ex-wives collecting alimony, a current one who likes to shop on Fifth Avenue, and four kids needing braces." He stood and paced the room aimlessly, more like a sulky teenager than a grown man. "Oh, I don't know. I don't know what to think. It was over two years ago and after her solicitor contacted me and I said 'no', I never heard from her again. Then I read she died, jumped off a roof or something. I thought it was over."

"Maybe one or both of his kids has got it in for you, ever think of that?"

" No, well, maybe. Maybe Cohen's girls have got it out for me. Maybe, from their point of view, I've done them wrong. But for God's sake, that was England. We're in America now."

"You ever hear of a boat?" Percy reached inside the breast pocket of her jacket and pulled out the letter sent to Felicity Dowell. She opened it up and handed it to him. "Miss Dowell show you this?"

He nodded.

"She says that's why you let her out of her contract."

He nodded again. "These letters don't have anything to do with the bad luck we've been having," Wainwright finally said, looking away.

"What makes you so sure?" Percy took the letter from his hand.

"I think it's Tony." He looked back at Percy again. "Or maybe he sent them. You want all the truth? This is it. If I wasn't locked into an ironclad contract with him, I'd get rid of him. Tony likes to flaunt his position as 'one of the world's leading actors'. He scorns the traditions of the theatre, despite his recently acquired title. An East Ender is always the same, spoiling for a fight. I don't put anything past him. He's a power-hungry prick."

"Don't hold anything back," remarked Percy.

"He's been walking around backstage saying the name every chance he gets." Wainwright went on like a burst dam spewing words instead of water. "Once he stood in the middle of the stage, begging the curse to rain down on him. That's when the sandbag fell on the stage manager. Tony had been standing in the same spot only moments before. I think he rigged it and it was a joke gone awry, but he still won't stop. This morning the police found a microphone near stage left with a wire going up to the catwalk. There was a loud speaker up there. That's where all the moaning sounds were coming from that were throwing the actors off. They're running fingerprints on it, but I know it was Tony."

"Sounds like he's trying to close the show. Why would that be?"

Wound down, Wainwright dropped into a chair, his air of self-righteousness leaving him completely. "He...he wanted to produce the Scottish play himself. In fact, he was in the middle of mounting it but went into heavy debt when he lost a bundle playing the horses at Kempton Park. I offered to cover his losses, if he'd step aside and let me have this production. He didn't want to but he had no choice. He'd already had a 'conversation' with someone about breaking his legs. The Brits aren't any different about gambling debts than us Yanks."

"They just do it after tea?"

He let out an appreciative chuckle. "I understand he's recouped his losses now, but it's too late. We have an ironclad contract and I'm not letting him out."

"If he keeps the show from opening, he can come back later with his own money and do it his way?"

"Yes, it's extreme but possible. I don't have to tell you, the money in a hit is on the producer's end. Tony makes a good salary, but nothing like he would make if he was still producing it, too." He threw his head back and closed his eyes. "Jesus, it's like everything that can go wrong, has gone wrong. Maybe we are cursed." He opened his eyes. "About Stars and Stripes Forever, I didn't mention the…the…little trouble to you because I wanted to let sleeping dogs lie. And I don't need the publicity over it. It's an all-American family show. I need people to think I'm a good guy."

"There's a stretch, but good for you if you can pull it off." Percy walked to the door, opened it, and turn back. "Now that we're

done here, I'm going undercover to learn how to be an assistant stage manager. Pop is nosing around on some other angles while I'm doing this. That makes two of us on this case, but I'm giving you a break. Both of us for twenty-five bucks a day, plus expenses. You going to have a problem with that?"

Wainwright, jumped in saying, "None whatever. Pop helped me out of a blackmailing scheme when I was starting out--"

"I have no doubt."

"So I want this cleared up as soon as possible, but…" He hesitated going on.

"What?"

"A good ASM is the stage manager's right hand man. They both are crucial to the running of a big show like ours.

Dozens of light, sound, and placement cues going on at the same time, sets coming in and out. You can't just walk in and --"

"Sure I can, Wainwright. Price of all your troubles. You had a 'good' ASM and now you've got me." She banged the door behind her on her way out.

I can't believe I thought that idiot was remotely attractive. Never judge a book by its cover, Percy. Words to live by.

Chapter Sixteen

Percy turned around and bumped into a man an inch or two shorter than she was. He looked at her with a leer and grabbed both her arms with his beefy hands.

"Afternoon, Sir Anthony," she said, pulling back, with a slight smile. "Want to let go?"

"And you are, my dear?" The man, reeking of alcohol and wearing a five o'clock shadow, continued his hold on Percy's arms. "An Amazon warrior? A goddess of Zeus? A larger than life package of womanliness for only the likes of me?"

Oh, jeesh, what a ham.

She broke free, studying his demeanor. Something was out of sorts. This was a man pretending to be a rakish charmer, and missing by a New York Yankee mile. "None of the above. I'm the new ASM. Name of Persephone Cole. You can call me--"

"Persephone," he interrupted, saying each syllable with distinction. He stepped forward again, his foul breath making her eyes water. "So I was right. The daughter of Zeus and Queen of the Underworld. A perfect foil for me. I--"

"Yeah, yeah, back off, tiger. And I'm only going to tell you that once," she warned. She lightened her mood instantly. "As I was saying, *Sir* Anthony, I hate to rush off, but I'm the new assistant stage manager and I have a job to do." She looked over his shoulder at Kyle, drumming his fingers on his podium some ten feet away, looking angrily at her.

"So see you around." Percy flashed him a smile. She moved around the burly actor and took a step toward the waiting stage manager.

"That's too bad, my fiery dove," Sir Anthony replied, disappointment coating his words. "I was hoping to invite you to my dressing chambers for a little 'cheer' and chat."

She spun around and took him by the arm saying, "On second thought, I always have a moment for the star of the show, Sir Anthony. Now where's your dressing room?"

"Right over here, my dear." He pointed to a door at the back of the stage with a red painted star over his stenciled name. He pulled her toward it.

As they passed a fuming Kyle, Percy shrugged and gave her new boss a 'what can you do?' look.

"Back in five minutes." She removed her fedora and tossed it on the edge of the podium. Red curls cascaded down her back and shoulders.

The actor pushed open the door and escorted Percy inside a lavishly decorated room fit for a Broadway star of his stature, carrying the scent of expensive leather and a man's sultry aftershave.

Freshly painted white walls displayed framed reviews, pictures of celebrities, and posters of productions in which Sir Anthony had starred. Along one wall, a small brown leather couch sat holding a curled up, sleeping cat. A light brown fur throw was draped on one armrest; a throw pillow leaned against the other. In front of the sofa a gleaming walnut coffee table rested, laden with books and scripts, tidily piled on one end. A matching leather chair sat to one side of the sofa, wearing a pillow in the same fur as the throw.

Vases of different types of flowers, some local, some exotic, topped every available surface of the room. The worn tile floor was covered with a zebra rug, Percy guessing it was real, probably shot by Ernest Hemingway, pictured in one of the photos.

On another wall and next to a built-in sink, was a small make-shift kitchenette. To the left of the sink, a similar refrigerator to Wainwright's sat in the middle of a rectangular table. Next to the tiny refrigerator was a hotplate. Off-white coffee mugs and dishes, cooking utensils, and silverware were stacked neatly beside it. The stack was topped with a folded dishcloth. The opposite end of the table held half-filled liquor bottles, glasses, and a silver ice bucket. Against the remaining wall was a dressing table with a large mirror. Telegrams and cards were laid within the four sides of its frame in an orderly fashion.

Either this guy is very neat or he's got a butler. I'm voting butler.

"Come in, my fiery Persephone, and sit down." He smiled a cat-got-the-canary smile at her. "Make yourself comfortable." He gestured to the sofa.

He must be kidding.

Ignoring him, she walked over to the dressing table and leaned against it. "Nice digs. Who does your decorating?"

Sir Anthony crossed to the sofa, picked up the sleeping cat, and sat down setting the cat in his lap. The animal's fur was almost as white as the walls, except for the legs, face, ears, and tail, which wore a rich dark brown. The exotic feline yawned, circled and lay down again on the man's lap. Stroking the cat, the actor looked up at Percy with a smile.

"I have a man who travels with me."

I knew it.

"He's a bit of a stuffed-shirt, but faithful. This is Ananda Mahidol. I call him Anny." Sir Anthony gestured to the sleeping animal. "He's named for the King of Siam, who gave him to me."

"What kind of cat is it?"

"A Siamese. I think he's one of the few in America. I had to pay a fortune to get him into the country, but I don't travel anywhere without Anny." He lifted the cat, kissed it several times on the top of the head then returned it to his lap, where the actor continued the stroking session.

"Uh-huh. Well, he's a cutie. So I understand this production of Macbeth was once yours," she said, getting right to it. "You sold off the rights to Wainwright or something like that."

The smile faded from the actor's face. He stood, returned the cat to the sofa, and crossed over to the liquor and began to fill a glass with ice from the bucket.

Percy went on, "Some people are saying you like to play pranks; that you're responsible for what's been going on around here."

Sir Anthony wheeled around so quickly, an ice cube flew out of the glass. "I think you should leave, young lady. I want to be alone."

"You saw how far that got Garbo, so forget it." Smiling, she went to him and took the glass from his shaking hand. "Besides, you offered me a drink and I'm going to collect." She poured herself a large whiskey, crossed back to the dressing table and set the glass down, untouched. A stack of playing cards on the coffee table attracted her attention. "I understand you're a gambling man, so I'll make you a little wager. I'll bet you know something about Carlisle being here until midnight last night."

The man visibly shuddered before trying to recover. He became the caricature of a haughty Englishman before saying, "What makes you say that?"

"Just a hunch." She reached inside her pants pocket and pulled out the bag of pistachios. "Want a nut?" He shook his head. "Good, more for me. Okay, so one, I understand you're at the theatre all hours playing cards with the boys and two, you've been drinking. You're known for never touching the hooch before a show and yet here you are, boozing it up.

There must be a reason." She pointed a finger at him. "I think you saw something last night." She grinned at him.

"Who are you?" he demanded. "You don't sound like any ASM I've ever known."

"I'll make you a deal. You tell me what I want to know and I'll tell you."

His eyes narrowed and he stood up to his full five-foot ten inches, looking every inch the Scottish king. "Wainwright sent you, didn't he? That prick. He wants to see me off the show, that miserable pr--"

"Yeah, yeah," she interrupted. "'Prick', I got it. Everybody's a prick around here. But he seems to have good reasons for wanting you gone. You keep doing not so funny practical jokes, like moaning sounds coming from a loudspeaker on the catwalk. The catwalk from which Carlisle fell to his death. Doesn't make you look too good."

"The police already questioned me about that." His famous rumbling baritone voice became shrill. "Rudy Carlisle is the one who put it up there for me. Have you seen those rails up to the catwalk? I couldn't climb those if my life depended on it. Bad knee."

"Now why would he do that for you?"

"Let's say he was a better actor than card player. He was settling a debt." The actor relaxed a little, and sat down beside the cat, stroking the animal's head with the index finger of his hand.

Percy heard the cat purring from across the room.

"Very soothing that," the actor said, looking down at the cat. "The purr of a cat is the most tranquilizing sound in the world."

"What happened last night?" Percy's voice was gentle, as soothing as she could match to the cat's purr.

She watched him as he stroked the cat, waiting him out. Finally he began to speak.

"You're right. We were playing cards last night, just Rudy and me. He was trying to recoup some of his losses. I let him win something back and he decided to leave. It must have been around eleven-thirty. We said good night and he went on his way. I asked him to leave the door slightly ajar. Sometimes I like to circulate the air, but I only do it when I know Anny is sleeping and won't try to get out. About ten minutes later I heard voices, two, echoing from somewhere out on the stage. I couldn't make out whose voices they were, but they sounded angry, combative.

"Two men, a man and woman, what?"

"I couldn't tell; it was all distorted by the time it got to me. I rose from my dressing table and went to the door, just when there was this bone-chilling, blood-curdling scream." The look in his eyes got far away, as if he was reliving the moment. "I ran out to the stage following the sound, and saw Rudy lying in a heap on the floor, his body all mangled and bleeding. I knew in an instant he was dead. I've seen enough of it during the Blitz."

"What did you do then?" Percy prodded in a half whisper.

"I…I…heard someone descending the rungs from the catwalk. It was so dark, I couldn't see anything. I panicked. I backed away and hurried to my dressing room, as quietly as I could. I locked the door and stayed here all night until the police arrived this morning. I don't think he saw me. And I certainly didn't see whoever it was coming down those rungs. That's what I told the police and that's the truth.

"You said 'he'. Are you sure you *couldn't* tell if both voices were men?"

"I can't say. In thinking it over, I realize one of the voices was more in a softer, monotone, but the second was loud and aggressive. I think the second voice was Rudy's, but to be honest, I can't say for sure. It was too distorted. The other voice could have been a man or a woman." He looked at her in a sincere manner. "The police believe me, you know. They know it wasn't me who pushed Rudy from the catwalk."

"That's what they want you to believe, for the moment. If I was you, I'd have a good lawyer at hand. Or do you call it a solicitor?" She popped a pistachio in her mouth. "Cops tell you not to leave town?"

He sat up erect and proper. "I told them I couldn't leave town, anyway. I have a show to do. Eight performances a week."

"Speaking of that, I'd better get going." Percy looked at her watch. "I've got a job to learn." She opened the door to his dressing room.

"Hey!" he said, as she breezed out the door. "You didn't tell me who you are and what you're really doing here."

She turned back to him, hand still on the doorknob. "Like you said, I'm fiery Persephone. Don't get too close or you might get burned." She laughed as she closed the door.

Chapter Seventeen

Elsie, I've seen the woman detective. She looks bovine and lazy. I don't think we have anything to worry about with her but we have something much more important with which to deal. Laverne came to me this morning. She said Carlisle told her he was watching us. She wants money to keep silent, even though she doesn't know yet who we really are. Respond to this as soon as you can. I will be looking for your answer.

Evelyn.

Chapter Eighteen

Percy headed for the stage manager's podium and noticed Kyle's girlfriend, the assistant wardrobe manager, had joined him. Heads together, they seemed serious and intimate, talking in low, hushed tones. When they heard her footsteps, both heads snapped in her direction, her blue eyes and his brown riveted on her. The girl nervously tugged at the collar of her blue smock, turned and hurried away, waist length, light brown hair reminding Percy of Alice in Wonderland just a little. *That's right. Her name is Alice. Very apropos.*

"It's about time you showed up here." Kyle's tone was peevish, as if he couldn't wait for her to get into earshot. A good looking young man, if on the short side, his dark eyes flashed at Percy in annoyance. He tossed his dark head like a frustrated horse that had been waiting at the gate too long. Searching through papers, he gathered them in a pile. He handed them to her, and topped the pile with a stapled three-page, single-spaced typed document.

She took the papers and removed the top document without saying a word. She heard a clanking sound of an electrical switch being turned on. A minimum of lighting came on in the theatre.

"Where'd that come from?" Percy pivoted her head toward the sound.

"The light box is over there." Kyle pointed to an off-stage metal box on the wall. "It must be one o'clock. Hal turned the work lights on. Nobody else is allowed to touch that box. Remember that."

"Got it. Who's Hal?"

"Head of Lighting. His office is in the basement."

Percy glanced around. Although the lighting was flat and in some places almost nonexistent, the entire backstage area was marginally lit, unlike before.

"You're name's Percy, isn't it?" His mood had softened somewhat and he smiled.

"It is. And you're Kyle."

"Mavis has given me a W-Two form for you to fill out when you get a chance, but let's do that in between shows. Agreed?"

"Yeah."

"Good. That list is the order of when you do parts of your job. See?"

Percy nodded, angling the document toward the small but strong covered-light taped to his podium.

Kyle tapped a line of the paper with his finger. "The first thing you do when you arrive one hour before the show, which is one p.m. matinee days and seven o'clock in the evening, is to check in with me. If there are any changes, I'll let you know."

"Changes? In what?" She looked up into his face.

"Changes in cast, wardrobe, scenery; if any equipment is malfunctioning, things like that." His tone was impatient. "Haven't you ever done this before? Wainwright said you know what you're doing."

"Yeah, I know what I'm doing." Her answer was a little too gruff. "Each show is a little different, that's all," she added in a softer tone.

"All right." He appeared to be somewhat mollified. "Then you check in with the prop master, the wardrobe supervisor, hair and wig stylist to see if they have any problems they need settled. If they do, you come to me, and I settle them."

Letting me know from the git-go who the boss is.

"That should take you to half-hour. At half-hour you do the usual knock on the dressing room doors to make sure everyone is in and accounted for and you check them off. Look at the bottom of this stack," he said grabbing the pile from her hands. "Here is the paper with the names of every cast member. There are thirty, eighteen men and twelve women."

"That's an interesting ratio. I didn't think there were so many women in his plays."

"With the war on, we have a dearth of men. Most are playing ten, fifteen years younger and some of these so-called actors wouldn't be able to step foot on a stage in ordinary times. We have even more women, if you count the crew. Many of the walk-on roles
and foot soldiers are played by mannish looking women. Brenda could double as a Sumo wrestler. Then there's the tall ones, like
yourself. Except for Alfred. He's playing the tall witch until they can find somebody. I understand they offered you the part."

"No." *Boy, half-truths and rumors spread like wildfires back stage. Like a lot of other places.*

"Alfred did the role in summer stock, he says." Kyle went on, as if Percy hadn't replied. "Speaking of the Weird Sisters --"

"I didn't know we were," interrupted Percy. "Tell me though, why aren't you in the service, a fine looking example of manhood like you? You're old enough. How old are you?"

Kyle blushed and swallowed then looked away. "Not that it's any of your business, but I have a heart murmur."

"Ah! Sorry." Percy smiled in what she hoped was a disarming manner. "Any chance you want to become an actor? I hear there's a production with a dearth of men."

He returned her smile for a moment. "I prefer backstage. Now where were we? Oh, yes, this is important and a major part of your job. On both sides of the stage are platforms on wheels. Come with me; I'll show you." He hurried along and Percy followed him about twenty-five feet back to the last entrance and exit wing delineated by the velvet curtains. "See that?"

He pointed to a contraption that looked straight out of the dark ages. A rectangular wooden platform was elevated about twenty feet in the air and sat on a wooden frame supported by three crossed two by fours forming 'Xs' in the center. The frame sat on another platform at the base attached to four large wheels, two in the front and two in the back. One end of the top platform extended out from the frame by about ten feet and onto the stage. A set of stairs ran up the other side to the top. The whole thing looked like a movable diving board for a pool only there was no water. Percy was glad she was not playing one of the witches.

"There's one just like it on stage right," Kyle said. "Once up there, the Weird Sisters are rolled on and off the stage by the stagehands. The witches are behind most of the scenes taking place on stage. Their costumes are cumbersome, as you will see. Your job is to help the three witches get up and down the stairs, and to let the stagehands know when it's time to roll the platform out onto the stage and pull it back again. See that white line?" He pointed to a painted line running down the side of the platform. "It shouldn't be
pushed out any farther into the sightlines than that. The cues for moving the platforms are written on the last piece of paper.
Memorize them. The actors say their cues fast and you don't want to get it wrong."

He pivoted and walked across stage. "Let's go to the platform on the other side, so you can see it for yourself. It's a duplicate of this one. The wheels are kept locked so it doesn't slide onstage when it's not supposed to. It did that once in rehearsals." Kyle let out a chuckle and Percy dutifully chortled, too. She walked behind him across the sixty-five foot wide stage and glanced out at the empty house once more.

This is the spookiest place I've ever been in, and I've been in some pretty spooky places.

Unaware of her discomfort, Kyle prattled on. "So, after you check in all the actors and let me know who is absent, if any, then you go back to props and help Ralph set up the battle equipment, the armor, helmets and swords."

"Are they real?" Percy was surprised. This acting business sounded more dangerous by the minute.

"No, of course not. Paper Mache, mostly. Except for two of the daggers and Sir Anthony's paraphernalia. He said his had to be real, so we bought a set from an English earl who fell on hard times. And the daggers are very real, as they are almost characters in the play."

Percy was maybe half way across the stage, when she came to a stop. "Wait a minute. What the hell is that?" She pointed to the top of the platform at stage right, barely visible in the poor light.

Kyle paused, turned, and followed her pointing finger. "What?" But he was too close to the platform and too short to see the top of it. "What? What is it?"

Percy didn't answer, but dropped the papers and started running, passing the bewildered stage manager. She dashed to the other side of the platform, ignoring a sputtering Kyle, and took the steps two at a time.

"Holy Toledo," she cried out, moving forward as fast as she dared on the narrow platform. She dropped down on all fours and crawled out until she could grab a still hand extended above the inert body of a woman. As she got closer, her knee hit something hard and sharp. She looked down. A lethal dagger, metal glittering in between streaks of blood, lay on the platform.

Kyle clamored up the stairs, but she didn't turn to face him. For a moment there was silence, as if he had frozen in place when he saw the horrible sight.

"Oh, my God! Who is it?" He moved forward close enough to the kneeling Percy to see the face of the fallen when he leaned over. "Oh, my God, it's Laverne. Is she…?" He couldn't finish the sentence.

"No! She's alive! She's unconscious, but I can feel a pulse. Call an ambulance." Her voice was cool and calm, unlike how she felt inside. "Then make another call to the cops. I'll stay here to see if I can help." She looked up into his drawn face. "Hurry!"

Kyle nodded, his jaw working and his lips pinched together. He wheeled around and disappeared back down the stairs. She could hear the echoes of his footsteps running to the only pay phone backstage or maybe the producer's office. The sounds tapered off and the theatre became eerily quiet again.

Percy reached into the pocket of her jacket and bought out a small but powerful flashlight, one she was never without. Turning it on, she inspected the woman without touching her.

Laverne, face half hidden by tangled hair, lay on her back with one arm flung over her head, the arm Percy had taken to feel a pulse. One leg was out straight, the other bent, toes touching the knee of the straight one. She had fallen in such a way, she'd almost covered the width of the platform on which she lay. There was wet blood everywhere, in particular on the abdomen and surrounding platform, already soaking into the wood.

After finding the approximate location of the knife's penetration, Percy ripped off her jacket, rolled it up, and pressed hard against the wound with both hands. She'd read about soldiers dying on the battlefield not from an injury itself but from the loss of blood. Medics on the field were doing this new practice called a pressure point.

I don't know what the hell I'm doing, but maybe I can keep her from bleeding to death. Then I'll find out who's behind all this.

She removed one hand for a split-second to glance at her watch. One ten. She tried to ignore the blood on her hand, and returned it to the pressure point.

The ambulance and police should be arriving any moment. They'll be followed by the cast of a play that was not going to be performed today, if ever.

Chapter Nineteen

Persephone was fiddling with the key in the lock when the door of the apartment sprung open. "Man, are my dogs killing me," she said to whatever family member was at the door. "I must have been standing on my feet for the past four hours."

She looked into her father's face. His features were stern, eyes sad. A taut mouth replaced his usual smile.

"What is it? What's wrong?" Her heart raced. It was one thing to see tragedy on the job, another close to home.

Pop leaned into her, his voice barely above a whisper. "They delivered a telegram to Sylvia Rendell this afternoon. Her husband's missing in action."

Percy sucked in a startled breath. "Oh, Pop! Oh, my God, no."

Her mind flashed to an all too familiar scene up and down the densely populated block. Two officers, from whatever appropriate branch of the service, standing on the doorstep of a family's home delivering the news of the dead or missing. She reached out for her father's hand.

"How is Sylvia? Does Freddy know?"

"Not yet. Mother went and picked up the boys a couple of hours ago. They're in Oliver's room playing. Freddy's going to spend the night with us and Sylvia will come for him in the morning. She's over with her husband's parents now. I guess she'll tell the boy tomorrow. There's no rush on this kind of news."

Percy removed her fedora, ran fingers through tangled hair, and threw the hat on the rack near the door. "Let me go in and see how the boys are doing." She turned back to her father. "You're sure Freddy doesn't suspect?"

"I don't think so. They've been playing toy soldiers and now they're drawing their Halloween costumes. The winner gets to be the Green Lantern."

"What's that aroma? Doesn't have the pungent smell of Mother's milk fish stew."

"Sylvia gave Mother the pot of hotdogs and beans for the boys. It's on the stove in the kitchen."

"It's an ill wind that blows nobody any good."

"Persephone, behave."

"Sorry, Pop. Just trying to get rid of some of the tension with humor." She rolled her shoulders a few times. "After I see the boys, I need to take a quick shower," she said, knocking lightly on her son's door and opening it. "Then we can talk."

The two eight-year old boys were lying on their stomachs on the floor facing one another and coloring on paper. Either they didn't hear her or were so intent on their project they didn't look up.

"Hi, boys. Whatcha doing?"

Oliver looked up at his mother with a big grin on his face. Freddy glanced up and smiled, one of his top front teeth missing. The children could not have had more different coloring. Oliver inherited his father's fair skin, coal black hair, dark eyes surrounded by thick, long lashes, and a ready smile. He would be a heartthrob, like Leo the Louse, but unlike him, Oliver was sweet, kind and loving, almost to a fault.

Freddy had sandy colored hair, thin and straight, hazel eyes and freckles running across the bridge of his nose and spreading out to the end of his cheeks. They were both adorable.

And possibly, they're both fatherless, my child through desertion and Sylvia's child through war. Sometimes life just plain stinks.

"Hi, Mommy!" Oliver leapt up from the floor, holding his drawing. "Freddy and I are having a contest. The winner gets to wear the Green Lantern costume." He ran into his mother's waiting arms. Percy kneeled down and embraced her son, who whispered in her ear. "I don't think Freddy's picture is as good as mine, Mommy."

She studied her son's concerned face. "Did you want him to win, Oliver?" He looked away embarrassed then shrugged. Her voice was soft, as she looked over her son's shoulder to the child still coloring on the floor. "Well, you could both go as the Green Lantern in identical costumes. How does that sound?" She looked into her son's face. That wasn't the answer, she could tell. "Or you could say you've decided to go as something else, like a pirate."

Oliver's eyes got big and his mouth dropped open in pleasure and astonishment. "Could I have a parrot?"

"Not a real one, but we might be able to find a stuffed one or maybe your grandmother could make one out of all those feathers she's got in her sewing room. I'll ask her."

"What about a peg leg?"

"That would be more Grandpop's department, but I'll ask him, too."

Oliver broke free from his mother's embrace and ran back to his friend. "Freddy, I'm going as a pirate!"

Freddy looked up, his face frozen in a similar look of joy as Oliver's. "Wow! Like Bluebeard?"

"Uh-huh," Oliver answered enthusiastically, nodding his head. "With a parrot and everything!" He threw himself down on the floor and snatched for a clean piece of paper. "I'm going to draw it. You can have the Green Lantern," he said to Freddy, as an afterthought.

Percy turned to leave, but hesitated in the doorway. "Freddy." The small boy concentrating on his coloring, looked up, his face a question mark. "Freddy, this jack-o'-lantern that got stolen, was it carved and everything?"

He nodded in an animated way, only whispering a 'yes' before returning to his coloring.

"What about the others? Are all the other missing pumpkins carved, too?"

"Yes, ma'am. But mine was the best," he uttered with finality. "My grandpa helped me make it." Freddy reached for another crayon and returned to his project.

"Thanks, Freddy."

She backed out and closed the door, listening to the chatter of the two small boys. Exhaling a deep breath, she went down the hallway and into the kitchen. Mother was stirring something bubbling in a small pot on the stove.

"Hi Mother. Thanks for picking up the boys at Sylvia's and looking after them." She crossed over to her mother and stroked her shoulder. "What are you making?"

"Rice pudding for dessert, but I've thrown in those turnips about to go bad."

"Ah!" Percy's tone was noncommittal. "Any soda pop in the cooler?"

"No, Serendipity is at the movies with two of her gentlemen friends. They drank them when they were here."

"She's at the movies even though it's cooled off? It's supposed to be in the low fifties tonight," Percy said.

"The Rialto is having a Cary Grant marathon, starting with his first film with Mae West. You know, he isn't dead, just missing." She stopped stirring the pudding and looked at her daughter.

"Jeff Rendell, right? Not Cary Grant." Percy seized the least wrinkled apple from the bowl on the table. She took a big bite and juice ran down her chin.

"It's all very frightening, though," said Mother, returning her attention to the pudding. "I've suggested Sylvia not say anything yet to little Freddy until she knows more. It may all be a scare the child need never know about."

"Wise words, Mother," Percy said, heading for the swinging door adjoining the hallway and the kitchen.

"I didn't raise three children and not learn something."

"I'd say you learned a lot." *Just not about cooking.*

"Are you hungry, Persephone?" Mother spoke as if reading her thoughts. "There's still plenty of my milk fish stew."

"No thank you, Mother," she said, her voice laced with false regret. "I had something midtown while waiting to be interviewed by the police."

It was another one of her lies, a little white one, she liked to call it. She'd grabbed a hotdog from a vender outside the front stoop of the apartment building on her way up but was still starving. Maybe she could sneak off to the corner diner later for a hot plate dinner before it closed. This was chicken potpie night.

"By the way, I hope you haven't started on the Green Lantern costume. Oliver decided he wants to go as a pirate. Freddy's going to be the Green Lantern."

"I already told Sylvia not to worry about Freddy's Halloween costume, that I would make it. I'm half way through with the green one, but the boys are the same size. It won't make any difference."

"You're one in a million, Mother. Oliver wants to wear a parrot on his shoulder. I can work on that unless you happen to have some spare feathers you can stitch together by Halloween."

"Mr. McKlusky, upstairs, is a taxidermist, Persephone. Perhaps he has a spare one."

"Never know. But I'll deal with it later. Right now I have to have a talk with Pop. Business." As the door swung closed she heard her mother's voice.

"I'm going to call the boys for dinner now, but I'll save you some rice pudding, dear."

"Thank you, Mother."

She walked down the hall and into her bedroom. There she grabbed fresh clothes and headed for the bathroom and a quick shower. Not ten minutes later, she opened the door of the combination office, parlor.

The largest room in the apartment, the fifteen by twenty-five foot parlor was more Mother's room than anyone else's. It held pieces of her great-aunt's ornate furniture, each gilded within an inch of its life. Paintings of pastoral scenes and imaginary French aristocrats, Mother's plunge into the world of art, littered the walls. Another one of her hobbies gone awry, they filled wall space and brought forth much amusement, even from Mother. Except with her cooking, Mother was the first to admit a craft which eluded her, and painting certainly had. In sharp contrast, lush emerald green ferns hung in each of the large windows and other plants luxuriated on table tops, symbols of Mother's more accomplished diversion, her green thumb.

One corner of the room was given over to Cole Investigations. Pop was apparently listening for Percy to come in. At the sound of the door closing, she heard his voice from behind the two still-life peacocks strutting on the golden background of a pseudo Louis the Sixteenth room divider. That's where her father's dark oak desk and file cabinets sat. As a child, she knew of many long nights he sat working at that desk.

"Persephone, that you?"

"It is, Pop."

"I was just going over my notes." He came around the screen and looked at her.

"Child, say what we will about Mother's cooking, she does know how to sew," Pop remarked, when he noticed Percy wearing the orange, black and white Japanese print kimono Mother recently made for her birthday. She wore the robe over pajamas, wet hair wrapped in a thick yellow towel. Her father studied her face. "You look all wrung out. Are you sure you want to go over this tonight? It can wait until morning."

"It really can't, Pop." Percy threw herself down on the parlor's sofa, a comfortable-looking but faded brocade sofa with matching chair and ottoman dominating the section of the room nearest the door. A large and highly polished oak radio console sat next to one end of the sofa, Pop's pride and joy. A mock Tiffany floor lamp stood at the other. Percy reached up and gave the pull-chain a tug. Warm light flooded the room, helping to soften the day for Percy.

"Call it a gut instinct," she said, "but I don't think anything is the way it seems. We need to figure this out before more people get hurt. 'Fair is foul, and foul is fair'."

"Sherlock Holmes?"

"Macbeth."

"Doesn't sound good no matter who said it," Pop commented. "I called Mick at the station while waiting for you. He says the woman's going to make it. You saved her life, Persephone. She lost a lot of blood. Another ten or fifteen minutes and she would have been a goner."

"You're telling me. It felt like I got most of her blood on me. Is she awake yet? Can she talk?"

Pop shook his head. "Not yet."

"They might close the show because of this, Pop, and it's too bad. Riding back and forth on the subway I've been reading Macbeth. I haven't since high school. You don't appreciate it so much when you're a kid." She arranged several of the throw pillows at one end of the sofa then lay against them. "Oh, my aching back. I guess I'm not in as good a shape as I thought I was. Did I tell you about crawling down the side of that twenty-foot platform when no one was looking?"

Pop took on a worried look and sat down in a chair across from Percy, as threadbare but as comfortable as the sofa. "Persephone, I don't like you doing this type of work. It's not suited for a girl."

"Pop, I'd hate to be hanging by the neck since I was a 'girl'. Besides, now we can fix the fridge, buy Oliver a new pair of shoes, and maybe have a steak when this is over. More important, we promised to solve this. At least, I did and I mean to keep my word." The last statement sounded harsher than she intended. Percy picked the rest of her words with care, saying them with a smile, "I need your help with this, Pop. I hope we can be partners."

His face softened. "Well, I did learn a few interesting things, Persephone, and if we work on this together, I can keep an eye on you." He leaned forward and touched her hand lightly.

"Hmmm. That's good thinking, Pop, and along those lines, they're down two male spear carriers, one took a hike and the other is now one of the witches. I'll tell Wainwright you're about to join the cast as a replacement first thing in the morning. This way we can keep an eye on each other."

"I never fancied myself an actor, Persephone."

"I'd say, point your spear in the right direction and then follow it. Remember, Pop, there's no business like show business."

"You could have gone all day without saying that, Persephone. And I'd advise you not to do it again."

"Afraid I'll throw everything over for a life on the boards?" She laughed. "Fat chance. So what have you got, Pop?"

"First off, the knife or dagger. It was one of the two used in the play and kept in a locked box when not in use. But before and during the play, it's left out on the prop table. The Prop Master had laid it out around twelve-thirty today. Anybody could have taken it."

"Props is in charge of it, right? What's the Prop Master's name? Ralph somebody."

"Ralph Dunston. He's been doing his job for the past thirty-eight years. Ready to retire.
No reason it should be him. But he could be getting a bit sloppy."

"Or maybe scoring a big payoff to see him through his golden years. I'll check him out."

"How did you get so cynical, Persephone?"

"I had a cop for a father."

They both laughed.

"Did you know about the binoculars?" Pop looked at her with a grin, while she shook her head. "Hanging over the railing."

"There's no mention of them in the inventory list Mick gave to Mavis."

"Keeping them under wraps, Persephone. You know, you don't always want to tip your hand. Mick says they found a partial thumbprint on it."

"So maybe somebody's been watching from up there. I wonder what you can see. Or maybe it's a red herring" Percy mused for a moment.

"You mean, someone put the binoculars up there just to throw people off?"

"Or waste time."

"They're going to be fingerprinting the entire cast and crew starting tomorrow," Pop said.

"That'll take a day or two. A lot can happen in that time."

"But, if there's a match, it might solve the whole thing."

"Maybe." Percy let out a sigh, half from fatigue, half from sadness. "I don't know, Pop. 'Something wicked this way comes.'"

"Another ditty from Macbeth?"

"Yeah. Spoken by the first witch." She looked at her father. "Pop, you tell Mick about Bert's ex-wife back in Arizona?"

"Yes, he's going to have someone check it out."

"If Bert is there, I want Mavis to send him his pay, so I'll need to know one way or the other." She let out another sigh.

Pop patted his daughter's hand. "You're doing your best and then some. You can't take care of everybody, if that's what's troubling you."

Percy shook her head. "Not just that, Pop. I have a bad feeling about how all of this is going to play out. Not much adds up. I don't think this is about money. I think it's a vendetta."

"Those are the worst kind of cases, Persephone. No sense in them."

"I know."

They were both silent for a moment, each thinking their own separate thoughts.

"Before I tell you about Who's Who in the Theatre," Pop said, breaking the silence. "What's this about climbing down the side of a twenty-foot platform? I don't like it, child. I don't like it."

Ignoring his fatherly concern, Percy sat up on the sofa with renewed energy.

"What I found peculiar was the direction Laverne fell in, as if her attacker had been standing on the end of the platform and she came up the steps behind him. Might have surprised him in the middle of something. Or her."

"Maybe it was a rendezvous that went afoul."

"That's a possibility, too, but we're second guessing." She moved to the edge of the sofa. "Let's work on what we have and make a few conjectures."

"Conjectures? What's that?"

"A well-informed guess, Pop."

"In my day we called it a 'hunch'.

"Same thing. I got the term out of one of the law books Jude leant me."

"So that's where your brother gets all his five dollar words."

"We're getting off the track, Pop."

"So we are, Persephone. Go on with your conjectures."

"Okay. When Laverne was stabbed and fell to the platform, her killer would have had to run past the injured woman in order to get down, except she almost covered the entire width of the platform. And for the minute or two Laverne was still conscious, the killer never knew in which direction her body was going to spasm, possibly knocking him or her off the platform if they tried to pass. The killer had to get out of there before someone else showed up. Laverne can't have been stabbed more than fifteen or twenty minutes before I found her; she would have bled to death. It was a chancy act, probably spontaneous. What I think they did in order to get away was to crawl down from the side, sliding most of the time on the crossed two by fours to the floor, but I had to prove it."

"Why father's go gray," Pop remarked to himself, with a shake of his head.

Ignoring him, Percy went on. "After the paramedics took Laverne away, and the cops had examined the scene, I snuck back up when they weren't looking."

"Persephone, you know to never tamper with a crime scene." His tone was as sharp as it was shocked. Pop had been a cop alongside his brother, which led them to starting Cole

Investigations. Both had a deep respect for the methods of law enforcement.

"I didn't tamper with squat, Pop, and I was very careful not to touch or step in anything. Or tumble off the platform, either," she added. "When you look down, it's quite a drop. But, like I say, the killer had no choice. And it can be done. Especially if you're in pretty good shape and leave the dagger behind, which he or she did."

"How did you get down?"

"Three sets of two by fours are nailed together on the frame and form an 'x', one below the other. The frame juts out a good six inches more than the platform itself, probably for maximum support. I sat down, inched my way to the side of the platform, and rolled over on my belly. Then I put my feet down on the angled board of
the top 'x'. I got lucky; my rubber-soled shoes kept me from slipping. I dropped down, straddled the board, and lay flat on my stomach. Then I slid down to the first 'x', to where the two boards were nailed together. It was like sliding down a very narrow banister."

She leaned in to her father, who was listening to her intently. "Here's something that might help us out, Pop. I happened to look up and I barely missed a nail driven into the plank. A mistake, and I think carpentry just left it. Anyway, it came through the other side of the board by a good two inches. I reached up and touched it. It was sticky with someone's blood."

"That means..."

"Somebody has a helluva scratch on them, but whether it's an arm, torso, or leg, I don't know. Anyway, Pop, I used the next two crosses of the 'x' like a ladder. The whole process took less than a minute. So my conjecture is the attacker has a fairly serious scrape. If we can find out who that is, we might have our murderer. Tell me what you found out at the library."

Pop removed a small notepad from his breast pocket. "I wrote everything down. There was quite a lot, though with the war it hasn't been published for awhile, nineteen-forty, to be exact." He read through his notes at a fast pace. "The British producer, Jacob Cohen, Wainwright's partner for thirteen years." Pop looked up at his daughter. "Well-known for producing ballet and classical theatre for the past twenty years or so in the U.K. All started to fall apart when he was accused of being anti-Semitic, even though he was Jewish. Cohen came from a wealthy, upper crust family. His father was a member of the House of Commons, whatever that is."

"It runs the government over there, Pop. Winston Churchill was a member of the House of Commons before he became Prime Minister. Go on, what happened to Cohen?"

"This is the interesting part. If you read in between the lines of Who's Who in British Theatre, his death in nineteen-forty was listed as 'mysterious'. So I looked up back copies of the Guardian, a London newspaper. It had several articles on his death and I learned quite a bit more. It seems Cohen had an illness of an 'indeterminable cause' for several months before he died, which was suddenly at a late dinner. Keeled right over in his soup. The implication in the Guardian was he was poisoned, even though the police couldn't prove anything."

"What do you mean they couldn't prove anything? Didn't they do an autopsy?"

Pop shook his head. "The Jewish tradition is to get them into the ground as soon as possible, so he was buried the next day, with the doctor writing 'heart attack' on the death certificate. Two days later, the cemetery was destroyed in the London Blitz. Everything was blown up or charred to cinders. 'Charred to cinders'. Direct quote. So that just fanned the rumors already being spread by servants and locals that he had been poisoned. But nothing could be proved one way or the other. His wife had a nervous breakdown from it and was hospitalized. She threw herself off the roof of a sanatorium several months ago. Sad."

"Weren't there children? Two girls, I believe."

"Not much information on them, just their names and ages. Evelyn and Elsie, nineteen and seventeen. They were in boarding school at the time of their father's death. Didn't say where. That's about it. But back to Cohen's suspicious death. Rumors were flying around that Wainwright poisoned him to get control of a hot property called Stars and Stripes Forever. He was even brought in for questioning by the local bobbies, but like I say, there was no body, so no proof."

"Find out more about the girls, would you, Pop?"

"A conjecture or a hunch?"

"A thirst for knowledge. What else you got?"

"Dexter Wainwright, hit it big about when he became a junior producer with Jacob Cohen over in London. I remember him from before, and didn't care for him much. Known for stealing anything he can. He's been taken to court for plagiarism two times so far. He lost each time but never paid back nearly what he made. Must have a crafty lawyer."

"Natch."

"Married three times. His first to a theatre owner's daughter in Chicago. That's what gave him his start in show business."

"Did you find out anything about anyone else?"

"Sir Anthony. Nothing you don't already know, other than he is currently married to Wainwright's second wife."

"Are you kidding me? You know, his nibs is fooling around with the actress now doing Lady Macbeth."

"His wife stayed in London. Lord only knows what she's up to. About the director--"

"Hugo Cranston. Don't tell me he was or is married to somebody's ex."

"Not likely. He doesn't take to girls."

"So I understand."

"But he is in partnership with Wainwright on this production, a forty, sixty percent split; Wainwright having the lion's share."

"Another thing Wainwright didn't tell me. Where'd you read that?"

"Didn't. I overheard Cranston telling Mick at the station this afternoon."

"Good for you, Pop."

"Eavesdropping is one of those things comes naturally to a good P.I., Persephone."

"And you're one of the best. I wonder if those two have a 'You Die, It's Mine' clause."

"Right of Survivorship?"

"If so, I'd better keep an eye on our illustrious director for his own protection. That is, if this play can resurrect itself."

"Lots of 'ifs'."

The phone on the office desk and its extension in the hallway rang simultaneously. Percy looked at her watch. Eight-thirty. Father and daughter glanced at each other. Calls that late usually meant bad news.

"I'll get it, Pop. It might be the theatre telling me the whole deal is off. If that's the case, I'm only giving Wainwright half his money back, and he's lucky at that, the lying S.O.B." She rose and crossed to the phone.

"Hello? Mavis, what's up?" Percy listened for a moment then threw a surprised look to Pop, who'd been watching her. "Nine o'clock it is. I'll see you there." She hung up the phone and walked back to her father.

"Pop, that was Mavis making calls to the cast and crew. Wainwright convinced law enforcement that Carlisle falling to his death and Laverne being stabbed were accidents. The show goes on tomorrow as planned."

"I'll bet Mick's fit to be tied," Pop interjected. "But La Guardia's the boss."

"My call is for nine, rehearsal at ten, notes from noon to twelve-thirty, break for lunch after, and half-hour call is seven-thirty. All very orderly. Performance at eight, as usual. Sold out to a full
house; standing room only. There's nothing like the ghoulish appeal of a few deaths to pack an audience. Happy Halloween."

"A few? There's only been one death that I know of, Persephone."

"I'm counting the two elderly people who lost their lives in last week's fire. They may not have been in the theatre, but they're still dead."

"You think that's tied in?"

"I know it is." She stood pursing her lips, deep in thought. "Pop, I'd planned on being at the theatre at eight tomorrow and snooping around a little, but I think I'll take a trip back right now. I pilfered a key to the theatre before I left, just in case."

"Now, Persephone? It's going on nine o'clock. You've had a long day."

"I've got a feeling, Pop. Can't shake it. Mind if I take Ophelia? At this hour, the traffic shouldn't be too bad."

"Of course, but what are you looking for? Nobody's at the theatre at this hour."

"That's what they'd like you to think. I've discovered a lot of people can be there at all hours and no one's the wiser. I'll throw on some clothes, take a little spin, and watch the stage door for a little while. Maybe I won't go inside. I'll only be gone an hour or two."

"I should come with you, Persephone. Keep you company."

"Naw, don't bother, Pop. Let's just call this my little drive around Manhattan in the moonlight." She stood and removed the towel from her head, damp hair cascading down her back. "Tuck Oliver in for me, would you? Then go to bed. If I don't see you before tomorrow, you show up at the theatre at nine-thirty with pride. You're a spear carrier in a Broadway production," she joked.

"If you say so." He smiled, but added in a more serious tone, "Be careful, child."

"Always."

Chapter Twenty

What Percy hadn't admitted to her father was part of the reason for going out so late was to get another hotdog. If the hotdog vender was gone, maybe she'd run over to Loretta's Diner for chicken potpie. Luckily, Giuseppe was just closing up, and nice man that he was, he gave her two foot-long hotdogs in buns wrapped in newspaper for the price of one, mustard and sauerkraut included.

An idea came to Percy as she looked at the extra hotdog. She got into the car and instead of heading uptown, she made a slight detour a few blocks away to East Fourth Street. She drove slowly down the street, deserted except for a lone passerby and saw what she was looking for. Three small boys, ranging in ages from seven to eleven, stood huddled together on the sidewalk in the middle of the block. Flickering candles inside carved out pumpkins marked their spot on this chilly, dark night. Makeshift tables held a few other wares, probably also 'lifted' from the neighborhood.

Percy pulled over to the curb three or four car lengths away from them and thought about how to handle this. She vaguely knew the Carter boys, but she knew where they lived and heard their story. Up from the coal mines of Pennsylvania, their father had Black Lung disease. Their mother took in washing laundry. The five of them were crammed in a three-bedroom apartment with an elderly uncle. The boys were on their own most of the time, sad, skinny little boys who got into minor scraps more often than not. If things continued the way they were going, major trouble loomed in the not too distant future.

Next to the Carters, the Coles were well-off. It was hard to believe, Percy decided, but true.

Percy picked up one of the hotdogs and got out of the car, approaching the small boys. Even though it was in the low fifties,

they wore only tee shirts and ripped pants. In front of each of the jack-o'-lanterns was a torn piece of paper with 'five cents' scrawled on it.

"Hello, boys."

The three hadn't seen or heard her walk up and started when she spoke. The smallest one, hardly seven years old, appeared too frightened to move, but the two older one looked as if they might flee at any minute.

"What do you want? We ain't done nothing." The eldest, Bobby, gave her his best snarl. Fear and confusion overrode any threatening body language he used.

"You're Henry, Jaime, and Bobby, aren't you?" She gestured with her head from the smallest to the largest child.

"Who wants to know?" Bobby snarled again. Tough guy. Barely three feet tall.

"You know who I am. I'm Percy Cole, Oliver Cole's mother. We live over on East Houston."

"So?" This time the middle child, Jaime was the one who spoke. He wiped his nose with the bottom of his filthy tee shirt.

"So I'm here to talk about the jack-o'-lantern you took from our door. You're going to put it back, fellas, and you're going to put back all these others, too."

The smaller child, Henry, began to shake and tried to hide behind the middle brother, who brushed him away. "She's a copper. I heard about her. She's a copper," Henry wailed.

The other two boys froze in terror at the thought of it.

"Ah, they ain't got no lady cops," Bobby said after a time, blustering his way through his fear. He turned to leave. Percy grabbed the elder boy's shoulder. He struggled for a moment then went slack.

"You sure about that?" Percy's voice was easy but frightening.

"You here to arrest us?" Bobby barely whispered.

All three looked about to cry.

"No." Percy removed her hand from the child's shoulder. "I just want you to put this stuff back. And anything else that might have found its way into your jumble."

"We…we…" stuttered the middle boy, Jaime.

"You had any dinner?"

The change in subject confused the boys. They looked from one to the other.

"You boys up for a hotdog?" Percy drew out her penknife and set the foot-long hotdog on one of the makeshift stands.

The little one put his fist into his mouth and shook his head, huge eyes gaping at the food. The other boys stared into her face, as if trying to figure out why she was doing this.

She flipped open the knife and cut the dog into three sections, sauerkraut and mustard dripping from each piece. The three boys watched in silence. By the flickering light of a half dozen candles, she solemnly handed the food out to each boy.

"So kids, you put all this stuff back where it belongs, and I want it done tonight before you go to bed." She paused to run her fingers and penknife under a leaking fire hydrant next to her then pulled out her handkerchief, and dried her hands. "Then tomorrow, all three of you are going to go see Father Patrick at the parish on Fifth Street. You tell him I sent you."

"We ain't Catholic," Jaime said, in between bites. "Ma says we --"

"This hasn't anything to do with being Catholic. Father Patrick has a program after school and weekends for boys. It'll keep you busy and out of mischief, plus it's two squares a day, lunch and dinner."

"Ah, what's it cost?" Bobby shoved the last part of his share of the hotdog in his mouth. "We ain't got no money."

"It doesn't cost anything. But you're going to have to go every day. I'll check to make sure you do, boys." She raised one eyebrow, put her hands on her hips and glared at them. "And I mean every single day, starting tomorrow."

"Or what? You'll have us arrested if we don't?" Jaime shivered and gulped down the last of the food.

"Something like that."

The boys exchanged frightened looks then nodded.

"And remember, I know where you live. I know your names. I know *you*. Don't mess with me. You fold up your tents now and you put this stuff back."

"All of it?" Bobby looked around him in horror.

"All of it." Percy's voice was firm. "Just to help you out a little, I'll take ours back." She reached for the pumpkin with the crooked smile she helped carve, and turned in the direction of her car. She deliberately didn't look back.

Chapter Twenty-one

With the smell of the lone hotdog lying on the seat beside her, she pulled the car into a no parking zone several car spaces down from the theatre. She had a clear view of the side alley, lit well by streetlights. If anyone entered or left by the stage door, she would see them. Saturday night, nine-forty-five p.m. and Manhattan was bustling. Every other theatre up and down Theatre Row was open, one of them regurgitating patrons at the end of the shorter-spanned show, "Beat the Band." Well-dressed and lively people, chatted on the sidewalk as they first passed Ophelia and then the dark Royal Theatre, disappearing into various parts of the City.

Percy sat munching on the dog and staring at the narrow alleyway. She was having a lively chat with herself and not liking the outcome of the conversation.

What the hell are you doing here, Percy? Like the feeling of being a private dick more than the feeling of a pillow under your head? And you can't even leave the car without chancing a ticket or maybe having it towed by the fuzz. What an idiot.

Just as she licked her fingers clean and talked herself into driving home and going to bed, a thin, young man walked to the side of the theatre. He glanced around in a furtive way and darted into the alley. Catching a glimmer of his face, she recognized the man as one of the featured performers in Macbeth, Lennox. Percy looked at her watch. Nine-fifty.

The actors were sent home hours ago. I wonder if he forgot something. But he shouldn't have a key. If he gets in, that mean someone else is inside the theatre to let him in. Cast and crew were ordered to stay out tonight in no uncertain terms.

She pulled forward and saw he had, indeed, vanished inside the stage door. Putting the car in reverse, she backed up to her original spot.

Two or three minutes later, the young man emerged and walked quickly down the sidewalk in the other direction. Another theatre's show came to an end and a flurry of patrons passed her by on the sidewalk. This group was silent or grumbling quietly among themselves.

There's going to be a show closing soon. Too bad. More actors reading Variety or walking the pavements looking for a job. Oh grand, Percy, now you sound like you're in show biz. Pop was right. Watch yourself.

The crowd thinned out and an elegant, dark-haired woman walked toward her on the sidewalk, looking familiar.

Felicity Dowell. Out for an evening stroll at this hour or something else?

The woman, dressed in black with a cherry red scarf thrown around her neck, turned into the alleyway and disappeared. Percy didn't bother to pull the car up but merely waited where she was. Again, in less than three minutes, the actress came out, turning in the direction of her apartment.

Hmmm. Time for another chat with the former Lady Macbeth.

Percy started the motor and drove down the street, stopping at the curb several feet ahead of the walking woman. Motor idling, Percy slid over to the passenger side of the car and rolled down the window. She leaned her head out.

"Good evening, Miss Dowell." The actress started and nearly dropped her handbag. "Sorry. I didn't mean to startle you."

"Oh, Miss Cole." The actress forced a light laugh, bringing a nervous hand to her throat. "You did, though. Good evening." She began to walk down the sidewalk again.

Percy slid back to the driver's side, and depressed the accelerator slightly, keeping the car's pace the same as the walking woman. As she drove, Percy yelled out the open window. "Get in the car, Miss Dowell. I'll drive you to your apartment."

"No, thank you," came the prim reply, "I prefer to walk."

"I don't think so." Percy shouted and several people on the street glanced her way. "Unless you want a late night visit from the cops, get in the car. We need to have another talk."

Felicity Dowell came to a sudden halt. So did the car. The actress bent down and leaned inside the open window. "Just who do
you think you are?" Her voice was haughty and indignant. "I don't have to --"

"I'm the person who can give the cops the threatening letter somebody sent you," the detective interrupted at a more normal volume. "Plus certain other information. They *could* decide maybe you can't board a ship for England, maybe you need to hang around and answer some questions regarding a murder and an attempted one. You might be a witness, albeit a hostile one. But for sure, you wouldn't be sailing to join Lawrence Olivier in his latest project."

There was a moment's silence on both women's part. The actress opened the door, threw herself on the seat, and slammed the door. "What is it you want?" The cultured side of her voice turned into a guttural growl. She looked straight ahead.

Percy studied the actress's profile. "What were you doing just now inside the theatre? You've been gone from it for almost a week."

Flustered, the woman picked up her hand bag, opening and closing the clasp then fussed with the scarf around her neck. "I was merely out for a walk and thought I'd say hello to some of my friends. I didn't know the theatre was closed." She turned her head to Percy and allowed a smile that said, 'so there'.

"Cut the crap, lady, and don't make me mad." It was Percy's turn to growl. "Or I'm driving us to the police station right now and turning you over." It was a hollow threat, but Percy was always good at poker. She stared into the other woman's fearful eyes, the City streetlights allowing such scrutiny.

Felicity's jaw worked up and down, and she looked away. "I can't tell you," she murmured, in a teary voice.

"Sure you can. Just open those flappers and let her rip. I'm waiting." Percy spoke harsher than she felt, but if she needed to bully the woman into talking, that was just fine.

The actress sunk into the passenger's seat, covering her face with one manicured hand. She began to sob. "I...I had some bad news today. A dear friend died. I needed something to...help me through."

"Carlisle, right? I heard you were close. I'm sorry for your loss." She reached into the right pocket of her jacket and pulled out her handkerchief. "Here, it smells a little of mustard, but otherwise it's clean." She thrust the cloth into the other woman's hand. "Blow your nose."

"Thank you." The actress blew her nose delicately then folded the hanky into a square, and looked over at Percy. "I don't know that you're so tough. You're rather nice."

"Don't be fooled," Percy said, not making eye contact, but looking out the windshield's glass into the night. "I can be both. I can be neither. And I'm still waiting for an answer."

"You have to promise me you won't say anything to the police. I could be arrested."

"I can't promise you that. But I can promise that if it doesn't have anything to do with what's going on with this production, I won't mention your name."

The older woman turned a tearstained fact toward Percy. "Do you swear, Miss Cole?"

"Hey, I already gave you my word. So talk, already."

"Very well." She wiped her nose then sat up straight. "I was getting a supply of marijuana from Ned," she blurted out. "I go whenever I need some. He won't give me more than a two-day supply at a time. Sometimes not even that."

"Excuse me?" Percy's eyes got wide before she threw her head back and laughed.

"What's so funny?" Indignation overtook fear, as the actress challenged Percy with her question.

"Ned? Dealing drugs?" She continued to laugh. "Man, I never figured that in a million years. And you, a Viper."

"He isn't 'dealing drugs'. He merely supplies a few trusted friends with a gram or two."

"Oh, please. Spare me."

"And what do you mean, I'm a Viper? What's that?" Now anger seemed to replace the indignation.

"Just a term come out of Harlem for a pot smoker. So how does it work? How do you get a bag? The theatre is closed right now. How did you know Ned was there?"

Uncomfortable, Felicity Dowell ran a hand back and forth along the dashboard, concentrating on a nick on the glove box. "I…I…you have to come back after the show, when the theatre is dark. When I was in Macbeth, I would return about fifty minutes after curtain call."

"You turn in your dressing room key when you leave after each performance, don't you?"

"Yes, but Ned stays there. If you knock, he'll let you in. You buy it then."

"What kind of a knock? Not a regular one, or else he wouldn't open the door, right?"

Felicity Dowell didn't reply but nodded. After a beat, she said, "It's this." She fisted her hand and knocked seven times on the glove box, five fast raps then two slower ones. "Like that."

"In the states, we call that 'a shave and a haircut, two bits'."

The actress came to life and leaned into Percy. "You won't tell Ned, will you? I don't want him angry with me or..." She broke off.

"Cutting off your supply?" She shook her head. "I won't tell Ned who I got the info from." She let out a hoot of laughter again then sobered.

"Listen, Miss Dowell, I can't tell you how to live your life, but earlier today you said you gave up the booze. This weed thing, it's just another form of addiction, in case you didn't know. Of course, who am I to talk? I don't go anywhere without my pistachios. That's one of the reasons I'm a zaftig girl, as Mother would say." She pulled out the bag from the pocket of her jacket. "Have one," she offered.

The actress shook her head and looked back at the Royal Theatre. "To be completely candid--"

"Candid always works with me, so shoot," Percy interrupted, popping a pistachio in her mouth.

"I'm going to miss the play and being in America. If it wasn't for all this trouble and Larry being so insistent I return...but that's neither here nor there. In answer to your question, I don't think marijuana will be a problem for me in England. I don't even think you can get it there. It comes up from Mexico, doesn't it?" She looked over at the detective for affirmation.

"So you were turned on to it here. Interesting." She removed the shells from her mouth, opened the ashtray on the dashboard nearly overflowing with them, and dropped them onto the pile. "I'd better empty this ashtray soon," she muttered.

Percy turned back to the actress who was staring out the window at nothing. "Don't kid yourself. Even with the war on you can get weed anywhere. And a lot of it comes in from India in your part of the world. If you want it, you'll find it. The question is, do you?"

"I don't know," she answered, looking down but shaking her head. "I'm a weaker person than I like to think."

"Aren't we all," Percy replied.

"You seem pretty strong to me, Miss Cole. I envy you."

"Truth?" Percy turned the ignition over and started the car. "Every time I consider something like that, I remember my son. Any spare change I have, I'm throwing his way." She pulled out and drove to the actress's apartment, a few blocks distance.

"I don't have a son," Felicity Dowell said in a flat tone after they turned the corner.

"Then get a dog. Or a cat. I hear Sir Anthony is totally devoted to his." She glanced at the woman with a grin on her face.

The actress, at first wearing a surprised look, burst out laughing. "I like you, Percy Cole. At another time, we might be friends."

Percy pulled over to the curb in front of Felicity's apartment. "Have a safe voyage back to England, Miss Dowell. Try to stay clear of any jerry subs."

The actress got out of the car, shut the door, and leaned inside the open window. "Thank you. I'll have your hanky laundered and returned to you."

"Don't bother. I have a drawer full."

"Then I'll say goodbye, Miss Cole, and hope you solve your case. Put Miss Marple to shame." She backed up and waved.

"It's in the bag," Percy said, waving back. *I wish,* she added as an afterthought.

She pulled into the traffic, hung a u-turn, and drove back to the theatre. Percy parked the car in the no parking zone once more. She turned off the motor and got out, slamming the car door behind her.

If I get a ticket or hauled away, Wainwright is damn well paying for it.

Percy walked down the alleyway and rapped on the stage door with the signal. Ned opened the door, saw her, and with a shocked look, tried to shut the door in her face. Percy decided to strong arm her way inside.

No time for subtleties.

Ned stumbled back a few steps, as she barged through the door. He stared open mouthed at her.

"Hello, Ned. Fancy meeting you here. And at this hour." She wore a fake smile on her lips, but her eyes were hard.

He recovered somewhat and went into his small anteroom, shutting the bottom of the Dutch door behind him. "Hello, lady dick, what brings you here at this hour?"

"I understand you're selling something, something not quite so legal."

"Me? I ain't selling nothing." He picked up his well-read newspaper and sat on his stool, holding the paper in front of his face.

Percy leaned in and snatched the paper from his hands, throwing it over her head. "Here's the skinny, Ned, and I'm starting off nice about this. You're selling marijuana on the side, and I want you to stop. You're going to give me every gram of pot you've got, or I'm ripping you and this place apart until I find it. Now which way is it going to be?"

"You can't come in here threatening me like this," he protested, leaning forward in a confrontational way.

Percy took a step back, pulled the Dutch door open, reached inside and grabbed Ned by the collar of his shirt. She lifted his scrawny body off the stool, leaning her face into his frightened one. She could feel his feet kicking in the air.

"Maybe I need to make myself clearer. If you don't turn it over, when I get done searching through everything in this room and on your body, I'm hauling your ass off to jail for dealing drugs. You see if I don't. So it's me or the cops. You take your pick."

"Okay, okay." He waved his arms in surrender. "I don't have much left, that's all. I sold all but two packets. You can have them. It's not my fault," he whined, as Percy lowered him back onto the stool. "Don't take me to jail. I'm an old man." He reached in the breast pocket of his shirt, and pulled out two small, flat bags and thrust them at Percy.

Her eyes never leaving his face, she seized them with one hand, the other still holding onto the top of his shirt. "You got some kind of protection in here, Ned? 'Cause if you draw a gun on me, I'm going to kill you with it and there's a promise."

"A gun?" His face blanched of color. "There's no need for a gun. This is a friendly-like thing I do for friends I got in the theatre. Just a little extra cash, that's all, a little extra cash for my old age."

"Don't look now, Ned, but your old age is upon you and then some. You want to hang on to this job, your dealing days are over. You got me?"

His features scrunched up, almost as if he were going to cry, he nodded. "I thought you was my friend."

"In the long run I am. Who's your contact? How do you get your supply?" When he didn't answer, she shook him. "Come on, let's keep this conversation going."

He turned a reluctant face up to hers. "This guy from Harlem, he comes down once a week with a stash. He sells it to me for fifteen, I turns around and sells it for thirty. Everybody's happy."

"What's his name?"

"I don't think --"

Percy shook him again. "Name!"

"Reefer," Ned responded softly, looking away. "Reefer Jones. He specializes in marijuana. That's all I know. He's going to kill me if he finds out I snitched."

"He won't hear it from me, Ned." Percy released her grip on Ned, and he fell back down on the stool. She brushed at the wrinkles she'd made on his shirt. "Don't you worry about it. I'll take care of this my way. Everything will be copasetic. But you need to promise me you'll stop dealing, or I'll see to it you're not a happy man. You want to make some extra money, go work at Schraffts. You hear me, Ned?"

He nodded vehemently, whispering again and again, "Okay, okay."

"You sure you gave me all of it?"

"Yes, ma'am," he said, in a similar tone as Oliver. She bit back a smile.

"Then it's time for you to go home to your missus."

She stepped out of the small room and made way for him to get off the stool. Wordless, Ned scurried out, never looking her in the eyes. He opened the stage door, and without a backward glance, stepped out into the real world.

Percy sank down on the vacant stool and leaned against the wall, fatigue overrunning her. She leaned her face against the wall, which felt cool but unyielding. That was her sometimes, cool and unyielding. Aware of a large wall clock overhead ticking, she looked up and saw the time was ten forty-five. Yawning, Percy stood.

"No wonder I'm tired. Time to get home, kiss the kid goodnight, and call it a day. But finish the job first." She gave a good stretch and took her father's fedora off, throwing it on Ned's stool.

After checking the stage door to make sure it was locked, Percy made a quick but thorough search of Ned's small cubby hole. Satisfied it was clean, she trudged down the hall to the ladies room and flushed the two grams of marijuana down the john. Watching it swirl in the bowl and funnel into the plumbing system, memories of the past twenty-four hours swept through her.

Percy Cole, this has not been your best day. Terrorizing three little boys, threatening a nice English lady, and manhandling an old man. You should be ashamed of yourself.

"Oh, well," she said aloud. "That's show biz."

On the way out, she picked up her hat from the cubby hole and brushed it off, reshaping the crown. She plopped it on her head and stepped out into the real world, just as Ned had done. The door closed and locked behind her. Glancing back at it, she wasn't satisfied.

They need an alarm system on the theatre. This is ridiculous. People can come and go at all hours of the day or night. I'll suggest that to someone after this mess is over. If it's ever over.

The night was cooler. The temperature had dropped several degrees in the short time she'd been in the theatre and promised to continue its plummet. She buttoned her jacket and drew up the collar as she got into the driver's side of the car, realizing she hadn't gotten a parking ticket.

Maybe the day hasn't been so bad.

She thought about it, as she started the car.

Yeah, it has.

Chapter Twenty-two

The next morning was cold, less like autumn and more like winter. The heat wave had given way to a cold snap, temperature dropping from ninety-one degrees to thirty-seven in less than thirty-six hours. This severe type of weather didn't happen often but when it did, Percy's head ached. More like a tight band across her forehead, it was ever present and distracting. She'd read it had something to do with the barometric pressure, but whatever it was, she couldn't let it get in the way of the job. Percy exited the subway deep in thought.

A few of the trees had dusty leaves beginning to turn the colors of fall. If the garbage strike had been over, New York City would be back to normal.

Or maybe a garbage strike in Manhattan is normal.

Percy entered the theatre at five minutes before eight a.m. Ned's spot was vacant, but the Dutch doors were wide open. A small, overhead light showed on his empty stool. She reached inside and fisted a line of keys from the lower cubby holes. As she was more familiar with the theatre now, she knew these opened the prop, wardrobe, lighting, wig and hair rooms in the basement. She'd go there next.

The theatre was virtually dark, except for emergency lighting and the lone light center stage. Percy pulled the flashlight from her pocket and turned it on. While standing stage left in the open space, she studied her surroundings and listened intently. It was tomb quiet. Nothing moved, nothing sounded, yet Percy knew from experience that older buildings were filled with all kinds of creatures scurrying in hidden places. On occasion, there were two footed creatures, too, often much more dangerous.

She cast the light up toward the catwalk suspended thirty-five feet in the air. The breadth of the light widened until there was but the promise of illumination and nothing more.

'If it were done when 'tis done, then 'twere well it were done quickly'.

"Man," she said aloud, "I've got Macbeth on the mind." Percy crossed over to the column of rungs on the wall leading to the catwalk. Flashlight between her teeth, she grabbed onto the first rung and began the climb, never looking down.

Two minutes later and out of breath, she saw the underside of the four-foot wide catwalk. Passing through a small opening, Percy arrived at the top rung of the ladder. She extended her foot and stepped out onto the metal grating of the walk. As she tested it, it felt sturdy enough for her to relax a little. She loosened the clamp of her jaws on the torch, removed it from her mouth, and wiped off her saliva.

Ever the lady. I drool when I'm nervous.

Taking hesitant steps to one side of the walk, she grabbed the railing, noting it was only as high as her hips.

A person could fall from here with no trouble. They could be pushed easily enough, too.

Grasping the rail, she turned on her flashlight, and leaned over enough to see below. Clouds of dust particles moved lazily in the thin thread of her searching light.

Taut brown ropes hung like parts of a huge sailing vessel in the black vastness down to stage level. There the end of each rope attached to the pulley system controlled by stagehands. Where she stood, thirty-five feet above and running the length of the catwalk, the other end of each rope was threaded through large metal rings tied off with enormous hooks. These hooks held sandbags, and larger, heavier pieces owned by the theatre itself and stored for rentals. Seldom used, one even held a life-size wooden horse.

Beside them were the flies owned by Dexter Wainwright Productions, consisting of painted canvas backdrops of battle scenes, castle walls, interior rooms, faux stone arches, and bigger set pieces. These were raised and lowered during each performance for specific scenes. The ropes were labeled on the pulley system below with what they held in the stratosphere. Deceptively simple. Potentially lethal. The more she knew about show business, the more dangerous it seemed to her. Better to be a private investigator, headache and all.

Percy straightened up, took in a deep breath, and wished she hadn't. The air was dense, and dust filled, archaic smells of years gone by weighing it down.

Not for the faint of heart this catwalk, in any way, shape, or form.

She moved across the length of the walk with careful steps, looking for something but not sure what that something might be. As she hit the center, the walk began to vibrate, causing her to freeze mid-step. Instinctively, she reached out with her hands and hung on to both railings to steady herself. All thoughts of falling left her when she noticed the glint of something on the far wall near one of the rungs. Ignoring the feeling in the pit of her stomach, she hurried across what remained of the walkway. The closer she got to the end, the more the vibrating subsided.

Nearing the wall, she played her torch up and down in what she thought was the place she'd seen the glint. Perplexed, she dropped to her knees, ignored the metal grating that chaffed at them, and searched the wall closer to the floor.

About a foot and a half up, she found what she was looking for. A door handle made of painted-over metal. The location where the inside of the hand touched the handle was worn down to the metal from use over the years. In the dim light she ran her fingers over the seam of a short door, blending into the wall. No taller than two and a half or three feet, the door was nearly as wide as the catwalk.

What the hell is this for?

The handle turned easily in her hand. The silent door swung inward into dark obscurity. From a crouched position, she flashed the torch inside, and saw mounds of black and gray, in varying shapes and sizes, playing havoc with her eyesight and imagination. Nonetheless, she crawled inside.

Chapter Twenty-three

Evelyn, I got caught with the dagger! I didn't know what to do. First Carlisle was on to us and now his girlfriend. I didn't mean to stab her, I swear! I saw that detective woman come into the theatre snooping around. I'm frightened. We need to go home. Call me tonight. Evelyn, please. We have to talk about this. I think I killed her!

Elsie

Chapter Twenty-four

Percy sat several feet inside the darkened cavern of space, keeping the small door in her sights for a hasty exit, if necessary. She shone the flashlight above her and saw she could stand. She rose and slowly pivoted, playing the light up and down as she moved. The small room overflowed with wooden and cardboard boxes, once regal crystal chandeliers clownishly lying on their sides, parts of balconies resting against walls, even sections of stairs had been dragged in and were strewn everywhere.

Storage for stage pieces, but not from recently. Too dust-covered.

She began to relax, but continued to search the dark with her small torch, until she came to a figure.

A man! A man holding a club over his head!

She felt an adrenalin rush. Then her mind came back to reality. She moved closer.

You ninny, it's a human sized Statue of Liberty.

She reached out and touched the gray-green folds of the plaster dress, encrusted with layers of grime. "How the hell did they get you in here? They must have laid you on your side and gave you a good shove through the doorway," she said aloud.

She stepped behind the statue and ran into a card table. A kerosene lamp filled with the liquid sat at one end.

There's a fire hazard.

Percy ran fingers over the surface of the table. No dust. A fountain pen, tea cup, and lavender ribbon lay next to a small, yellow upright container, cylindrical in shape. She picked it up and twisted it around to read the label. It was emblazoned with a red skull and crossed bones.

"Rat poison," Percy muttered and shook it. The box felt nearly full. Nothing else was on the table. She returned the container to the table exactly as she found it, withdrew a clean handkerchief
from her pocket, and picked up the pen with it. Wrapping the pen with care, she stashed it in her pocket.

Time to leave. Get out while the getting's good.

Percy did a full one-hundred and eighty degree turn, patted Lady Liberty on the backside, and returned to the door. Down on all fours, she crawled through the opening and out onto the grating of the catwalk. As she reached back for the handle to pull the short door closed, she heard the slap, slap, slap of leather soled feet coming up the rungs on the far side of the catwalk. A slight echo followed each step, further announcing the approach.

Percy's mind raced as she closed the door with a near-silent click.

Whoever they are, they're nearly one hundred feet away. They can't see me in the dark and they won't be able to hear me going down. Thank God for my rubber-soled shoes.

She extinguished her flashlight, dropped it in her pocket, moved to her side of the rungs, and began to descend as quickly but as quietly as possible. She put out of her mind the thirty-five foot drop to the stage below as she placed one foot beneath the other on the metal rungs.

It's just a ladder, she kept thinking. *It's just a ladder.*

Once on the stage floor and breathing hard, she held on to the last rung and leaned against it, waiting for her head to stop pounding. Percy strained her eyes up into the vast darkness above, but saw nothing. There was the imperceptible sound of something up there, but it could have been her imagination playing tricks on her. An empty theatre inspired feelings of fear unlike no other place in the world, she decided, especially when a murderer was loose in it.

On the opposite side of the theatre than she'd started, she moved into the second to the last wing and looked across the stage at the platform on which she'd found Laverne. The top platform was now gone, having been ripped off and thrown away. The police felt it was no longer of any value to their investigation and you couldn't ask actors to step in the dried blood of one of their colleagues. Supposedly, a new platform was being built in the shop and would be brought here to replace the original in time for the rehearsal.

What the hell was somebody doing up on that platform when Laverne surprised them? How far away is that, anyway? The width of the stage is sixty-five feet, that's right. That's too far to throw a dagger. But midway. Hmmm. Maybe so.

Percy stepped out onto the stage and began to walk slowly across it, studying the floor as she went. It felt weird to be on an empty stage in front of an empty house, but Percy concentrated on something else. She paused midway in her trek across stage and squatted down. Amidst the scuffs and scratches on the old wood floor, she found fresh nicks and small gouges in the middle of the stage.

She ran back to where she'd come from, sprinted around the heavy curtains and into the last wing, the wing holding the second Weird Sisters platform. Up the stairs and to the 'diving' end of the platform she ran. Pausing, she removed her flashlight from her pocket and balanced it in her hand.

If I remember right, this weighs about the same as the dagger, maybe an ounce or two more. Close enough for jazz. Okay, toots, they say nothing can break this flashlight. Let's see if it's true.

And with that thought, Percy took aim and threw it with all her might, aiming for center stage. Spinning through the air, the flashlight struck the floor with a thud then rolled a few feet and came to a stop.

I thought so.

Looking around to make sure no one was observing her, the detective dashed back down the stairs of the platform and across the stage to retrieve her torch. She tested the flashlight to see if it still worked. It did. Percy bent down and examined the floor again. She sat on her haunches and closed her eyes.

Percy envisioned what scenes took place in this spot. Many. This was a favored location of Macbeth to say his famous speeches or soliloquies. It was also a spot where most of the battle scenes took place. In fact, there were so many people performing here at certain times, if something got thrown, it couldn't help but strike someone. But was the dagger being practice thrown at someone in particular, like Sir Anthony, or at anyone who happens to stand here?

Good question, Percy.

Percy glanced up into the murky rafters again. Now that she knew what was up there, she could visualize the dangling scenery
and equipment some thirty or forty feet away. Another thought came to her.

There are two ways to drop whatever is up there on someone down here. You can cut a rope at the top or you can maneuver a pulley.

None of the ropes were cut that she'd been told. That meant whoever dropped the sandbag on the stage manager did it from below at stage level.

Percy stood, shook out her legs, and pocketed her flashlight once again. Single-purposed, she trotted across the remainder of the stage and to the outer wall where the pulley system lived. Ten feet away from this contraption stood the stage manager's podium. Traditionally he was the person who gave cues to the stagehands to raise and lower the pulleys. An important job, Percy decided.

No wonder a good stage manager is so well thought of.

Percy studied the pulley mechanism, probably ten feet high and fifteen feet in length. Attached to the brick wall, dozens of simple wheels with grooves along their outer circumference gripped the ropes from above. Below that, soldered rings on a thick metal railing held each rope securely tied, but within easy reach of a stagehand to either release or pull when given the cue.

All anyone has to do is walk by, reach out a hand and yank on a rope and something comes crashing down. It's taking a chance but, by God, anybody could do it. Especially when each rope has been so nicely marked for our murderer.

The stage door slammed, sending echoes of wood and metal banging against each other. The discordant sounds of two men talking and laughing rang throughout the theatre. She strained her eyes at her wrist watch and saw it was eight-thirty. Though it sounded like Wainwright and Cranston and she needed to tell Wainwright about his new thespian, she didn't want to see him quite yet. She still had work to do.

Percy backed away from the pulleys and snuck down the stairs to the basement. On the way down, she wondered what the producer and director had to be laughing about. As far as she could tell, they were on the brink of financial ruin.

* * * *

"What are you doing?" Percy wheeled around at the sound of a male voice sounding accusatory and self-righteous.

"You must be Ralph," Percy said with an easy smile. She put out her hand to the tall man, probably in his mid- to late-sixties, with

graying hair and deep circles under intelligent hazel eyes. His lanky frame matched hers in height but maybe only wore half the poundage.

"I'm Percy," she said. "The new ASM."

His demeanor and tone of voice changed instantly. "Oh." He drew the one word out, as he took her hand. "Sorry to sound so gruff. It's just with all that going on around here and I find someone fooling with the lock to the prop cage, I get a little nervous. Percy, is it?" He shook her hand amiably.

"Yes. I thought I'd come in early and check out my duties. I understand I'm supposed to help you hand out the armor and equipment to the actors for the battle scenes."

"That's right." Ralph stepped in front of her, retrieved a set of keys from his pocket, and with a practiced hand, unlocked the padlock. He flung the door open and reached for an overhead light. "Here they all are." He lifted a breastplate from a pile with one hand. Up close, Percy could tell it was a lightweight material and painted to look like metal.

"What's this made of?" She reached out and took it, expecting the body armor to be heavier. It weighed virtually nothing.

"Latex. And it's made from a mold. I prefer the paper machete, myself, although they weigh a bit more." He took it from her hand and turned it over. "See here?" He pointed to a white tape with a name scrawled on it. "Here's the actor's name, so that's who you hand it to when the battle scenes come up." He glanced closer to the name. "Never mind with this one. This was Carlisle's. I didn't remove the tape yet." He gave the tape a good pull at one end and it came off with a small ripping sound. Ralph replaced it on the mound with a tender hand. He looked at the neatly stacked piles of armor, helmets, breastplates, and swords. "We're running out of people to hand these out to. The next thing you know, they'll be asking me to put one on myself and run out on stage."

"It's a shame about the actor playing Macduff. That happen often around here?" She studied the elderly man. In her opinion he could no more climb up rungs to a catwalk than she could fit into a size twelve dress.

"Certainly not." There was a touch of insult in his voice. "Despite what outsiders think, the theatre is a cleanly run business. Oh, you have your hotheads and people who are in it for only the glamour or the money, but for most of us, it's the art itself."

"Wainwright in it for the art?" Percy made her way in between wooden sawhorses, stacks of books, lamps, and knickknacks to the back of the room where a locked glass cabinet sat.

"What Mr. Wainwright is in it for, is between him and his conscious." His voice became more reserved.

She turned and faced the man, trying for a disarming smile. "I only ask because I'm new to the theatre. I'm learning my way." She watched him thaw. *Man, a smile can get you a lot around here. I need to remember that for the future.*

"Of course, I understand. You have to ask questions. But let's keep it about the work itself, shall we?" He returned her smile with a genuine grin. Nice man.

"Tell me about this cabinet." Percy turned back to the glass and metal encased container. She pulled her bag of pistachios from her trouser pocket.

Ralph weaved through the props and came to her side. Both stood looking at the weaponry inside. He cleared his throat. "As you can see, this holds what we call hazardous props, like guns, knives, hatchets, things like that."

"Is this where the dagger that stabbed Laverne came from?"

"Yes."

"I see two of them still in here. Have a pistachio." She extended the bag in his direction. "Take two, they're small."

"Don't mind if I do," he replied with a laugh, taking a small handful. "Thanks. Regarding the daggers, we always have extras, in case one gets broken."

"Or confiscated by the police in a crime."

"I'll admit, that's a first for me." He cleared his throat again. "The two original daggers were from the sixteenth century, brought over by Sir Anthony. The one on the left is the reproduction I found in New Jersey. It can still kill a man though, original or not."

"I'll bet. Who has a key to this cabinet?"

"Right now, no one but me. When I found out the dagger had been taken from here, I changed the locks. Before, it was an old lock

and been on for years. Too many people had keys to it." He separated the shell from the pistachio with his fingers and ate the meat.

"Like who?"

"Like you, for instance, or your position," he added. "Plus me, my assistant, the director, the stage manager, and there was one hanging in Ned's room. A spare. It's not there now. So I changed the locks. I have the only key and there's an end to it."

"Pretty smart, Ralph."

He nodded and stood for a moment, staring into the case. "You know the difference between a dagger and a knife?"

"I do."

Ralph went on as if she hadn't spoken. "A dagger is a double-edged blade used for stabbing or thrusting. It's equally curved on both sides toward the point. A knife is any cutting edge or blade, handheld or otherwise. One side is curved and the other is the one for cutting." He turned to her, watching her stare into the case. "Which would you prefer to use? If you had to?"

"A gun."

Ralph threw back his head and laughed. "I like you, Percy. Percy." He mused for a moment, as he opened another pistachio with his fingertips. He seemed more relaxed. No more clearing of his throat. "What's that short for? Not Percival, that's a man's name. Persephone, perhaps? Daughter of the Underworld. Image doesn't quite fit you. Maybe you need to wear a Himation instead of pants." He threw the nut in his mouth.

"Himation. That's a long, woolen garment the women of ancient Greece wore, right?"

"Right."

"You sound like an educated man, Ralph."

"Harvard. Class of aught-five. But not for me. I've done pretty well here. Thirty-eight years and nothing like this has happened before. It was stolen from my prop room. It makes me look bad."

"Maybe that can be fixed."

He scrutinized her face. "You don't sound like any ASM I ever knew."

Percy walked around him and made for the door, saying over her shoulder, "We're a changing breed, Ralph. Thanks for the tour. I'll see you at the beginning of act one, scene two, to hand out the battle gear. Down stage right, isn't it?"

"Before then," he corrected, raising his voice to her departing figure. "We start handing them out when the Weird Sisters begin their first scene. The men need to be in place and ready to go with all
their props. And it's upstage right. There's a table I lay everything out on. You'll see it. Second to the last wing. The one in front of the witches' platform."

Percy stopped, wheeled around, and came back, leaning inside the door. "That's where most of the actors stand to enter the stage. Then the scene is done upstage center, right?"

"That's the place. Can't miss it. A lot of men in uniform," he said with a grin.

Percy thought for a moment. "Thanks."

Chapter Twenty-five

Elsie, the rooming house I'm staying in only has a phone in the lobby. I can't call you, someone might overhear us. We can't be seen together either, that detective is hanging around, looking everywhere. If she doesn't go away soon, I'll have to stop her. I don't mean to criticize, dear sister, but you may have made things worse by what you've done. However, there's no turning back and there's no going home. There is no home. Everything was stolen from us, including our precious mother, thanks to Dexter Wainwright. He will pay, but first he will suffer. We will make him and the rest of them suffer. We need to take care of Laverne. If she regains consciousness, she'll tell and then we will be finished. I'll bring the poison as soon as I can, but you'll have to do it. As lady Macbeth says, 'Screw your courage to the sticking place and we'll not fail'.

Evelyn

Chapter Twenty-six

"Care for some tea, Percy? I've brewed a fresh pot," Mavis said, with a ready smile.

"No, thanks. I've got a celery soda," Percy said, gesturing to the half-drunk bottle on her side of the stage manager's podium.

In the midst of the ordered chaos in the backstage preparation for the run-through, Mavis's calm demeanor seemed oddly misplaced. Stagehands whisked scenery from here to there or hammered last minute repairs on the Weird Sisters' platform. Actors scurried around in various stages of dress, makeup, and readiness. Director Hugo Cranston screamed out instructions to lighting men perched on tall ladders adjusting lights. Kyle, wearing a headset, repeated sound cues again and again from his podium microphone to someone in the back of the house. Everywhere people were either talking or yelling, and all were scrambling to be ready in time.

Percy found it hard to concentrate in the controlled bedlam, and she prided herself on being able to turn nearly anything off. But while studying the notes she'd gathered as she'd gone to each dressing room or department checking people in, she found herself going over the same things again and again. Still and all, she'd made a small amount of progress.

Not usually superstitious, she thought about the unlucky number, thirteen. Wainwright had been Cohen's partner for thirteen years. Thirteen women in the cast and crew were the right ages to be one or both of the Cohen girls.

Jacob Cohen's daughters being here was a long shot, she knew, but it was possible. She looked into the brown eyes of the producer's private secretary, a young woman on her list as one of the possibilities.

"Just let me know if you change your mind about the tea." Mavis smiled again. "I keep a pot going at all times in Dexter's
office. Go in and help yourself if you like, but mum's the word," she added, putting her finger to her lips."Don't tell anyone. We don't want the whole cast in there."

"I'll remember that. By the way, Mavis." Percy paused, looking in the stage manager's direction to make sure he couldn't overhear. "I want to see the original paperwork for every single hire, cast and crew, as soon as you can get it to me."

Mavis's smile waivered for a split second, while she digested this. "Of course, I'll put that together during the show. Will in between shows be soon enough?"

"That'll do. Thanks."

A departing smile flashed on the girl's face, as she turned on her well-shod feet and went back to the office. Percy noticed the flair of Mavis's skirt as she walked. A soft tan dress and jacket ensemble, fabric moving like heavy silk, was finished off by a string of pearls, no doubt real.

I saw an outfit like that in a fashion magazine at Gretchen's Beauty Parlor a couple of months ago. Cost a bundle. You don't get clothes like that doing any secretarial job I know, unless there's some extra-curricular activity.

"Excuse me, miss," said a voice she knew only too well, breaking into her thoughts. Percy turned, expecting to see her father. But standing before her was a short, dark haired man wearing pseudo battle armor from the middle ages, with scruffy eyebrows and an even scruffier beard.

So everything went smoothly with Pop's 'hire', Percy thought. *At least they can do something right around here.*

"I'd like to introduce myself." Pop stuck out a hand. "My name is Pop Parker, and I'm a new member of the cast." His blue eyes twinkled, the color emphasized even more by the blackness of the eyebrows and the red painted cheeks.

With a straight face, Percy took his hand and shook it. "I'm Percy Cole, the assistant stage manager. Nice beard."

"Glued on with some foul-smelling stuff called spirit gum," he replied. "Not sure it'll ever come off."

She fisted her hand and pointed her thumb over her back. "That's the stage manager, Kyle. I'd introduce you to him, but he's running cues right now with sound."

As if to prove the point, Kyle lost his temper as the sound of hoof beats came out of the loudspeakers. "No, no! It should be
trumpets," he bellowed into the microphone. "The battlefield trumpets. Cue number sixty-three is the battlefield trumpets. Let's start at the beginning, shall we?" His voice was menacing. "Cue number one, Act one, Scene one: A strike of lightening, and *your* cue is to follow with the roll of thunder. Cue number two…" He turned his head away and the rest was lost in the general hub-bub of the backstage noises.

"I guess I'll go and find out when and where I carry my spear on stage," Pop said in mock seriousness.

"Nice to meet you, Mr. Parker. Oh, here. You've got a loose thread." Percy leaned forward, pretended to grasp something on his shoulder, but whispered in his ear. "Be careful Pop. There's a lot going on around here, like falling sandbags, rat poison, and flying daggers. Keep your eyes open. Did you give the pen to O'Malley?"

Pop nodded imperceptibly.

"You tell him about Reefer Jones and to keep it up in Harlem?"

Pop looked at her and winked. "Mick's mighty grateful," he murmured.

"He should be," she whispered back. Percy straightened up and said in a normal voice, "There, I got it, Mr. Parker."

"Thank you, young lady." Pop turned on his heels and strutted away.

Percy watched him with a smile before returning to her list, hoping for a chance to make more sense of it.

"Percy darling," said a clipped British accent, interrupting her again. She turned to see the director fast approaching from another direction, this time wearing a yellow shirt and brown trousers, with a green, yellow, and brown tie nipping in his waist.

If I had a waist, I might try that look. Naw, too weird looking.

"I'm afraid we're going to have to use you to another advantage, apart from being the assistant stage manager," he called out to her, before coming to rest at her podium. "We're down two witches."

"Excuse me?"

A small woman, under five feet tall, trailed behind Hugo. She was done up like the scariest Halloween witch Percy had ever seen. The director turned to her. "Percy, this is Betty. She's the lead Weird Sister."

"How do you do." Betty's contralto voice was a surprising contrast to her size.

Hugo Cranston slapped the podium with his open palm and said in his best directorial tone, "I've decided you're to go with Betty. She'll show you where to stand and what to do. I've underlined the words that you say. Congratulations, you're witch number two."

"Excuse me?"

"Listen old crumpet," Hugo said, when he saw her reluctance. "This is emergency measures, probably just for today until we find somebody. We've got an ad in Variety. And I mean, you're perfect, a little overweight, but perfect. Such authority. I know it will transfer to the stage."

"But what about *my* job?" Percy stuttered, thinking that she'd lose a certain mobility backstage. "Who's handing out the props and helping the witches up and down the stairs?"

"My assistant will hand out the props. And you ladies can jolly well 'help' yourselves up and down the stairs." Hugo snapped at her with impatience.

"Come with me." Betty, grasped Percy's hand with her own miniature one. She dragged Percy away from the podium with gusto and toward lower stage left, where a large caldron awaited in the wings on an undersized rolling stage, called a platform trolley. The trolley held not only the black caldron, but imitation shrubs and canvas-covered rocks giving something of a semblance to a Scottish moor.

Percy pulled back. "Wait a minute. I'm no actress."

"Who cares?" With a strength the detective had no idea the small woman was capable of, Betty gave Percy's hand a hard tug. Off balance, Percy went flying through the air and tripped up the one step and onto the moveable set, regaining her balance by grabbing onto a prickly, fake bush.

"See in there?" Betty's cockney voice directed Percy's attention to papers taped to the inside of the enormous, round caldron. The witch hopped up beside Percy. "The whole scene is written out and all your words are underlined in red. If you get confused, say 'double, double toil and trouble' and tickity-boo, I'll take it from there. You see, luv, I can't be the only one standing on the stage. We're supposed to be the Weird Sisters, not the one weird broad. Alfred should be here in a minute. We'll run lines then."

"Alfred?" Percy studied the woman's face, encrusted with a long pointy chin with one large, hairy wart, a huge hooked nose, bushy, salt and pepper eyebrows and a scraggy wig. Even though her features were smothered in a nauseating gray-green powder, Percy knew this was an attractive young woman, early to mid-twenties, from checking her in earlier in her dressing room. Another of the thirteen possibilities.

"Alfred did the role day before yesterday," Betty went on. "Said he knew it from summer stock. Bollocks. The blighter just wanted to dress in drag, but the girl hired to replace him yesterday came down with the flu last night, she *says*. Malarkey. Once they find out what's going on in this cursed production of the Scottish Play, hardly no one wants to be in it, except for me. As far as I'm concerned, any place in America is better than going back to England with the war on, innit, eh? Like me mum says, take your refuge where you can get it."

Despite the turn of events, Percy looked at Betty with appreciation. Nothing seemed to throw her. Percy remembered the Prop Master's remark that things were getting so bad, someone might make him don a suit of armor and march onto the stage. Little did she know a version of that scenario was going to happen to her.

"So you're from England." Percy hoped to sound like she was making friendly conversation.

"That's right. Born and raised in East London, just like his nibs, Sir Anthony. Only I don't think I'm too good for where I come from. But it's nice not to be sitting in a bomb shelter, listening to the wireless for the next bombing raid. No clotted cream to be had these days, neither." Betty jumped from subject to subject with hardly a breath between. "We'll take you down to wardrobe and hair after we run lines. Shame to cover all that red hair with one of those wigs. They itch, too. Here comes Alfred." She pressed into Percy, looked up, and spoke quieter. "Try not to say anything about his false nose looking as wicked as mine. It's real, ducks, and he's sensitive about it."

* * * *

Twenty minutes later, Percy finished babbling assigned words written on cards placed within, under, and over props or hanging from various parts of the scenery. Progressing throughout
the script scene by scene, she'd said her few lines or stood ghoulishly in place on one of the 20-foot high platforms that would be rolled onstage behind the scenes during performance. It was a lot of standing. It was a lot of rolling.

Done, but by no means satisfied, she followed Betty down to wardrobe, thinking. *This show biz is getting dicier and dicier. I want to finish this job and get home to my son.*

Together, Percy and Betty stood to the side, waiting for their turn with Kyle's girlfriend, Alice, for Percy's costume. Betty tugged on Percy's shirt sleeve and the taller woman bent down within ear shot.

"The supervisor is out in the house, taking wardrobe notes from the director. Alice is in charge now, which is no picnic, luv."

Together they watched as the wardrobe assistant, wearing the familiar blue smock, handed out different Tartan kilts to the supporting actors for the run-through in a dismissive manner. Percy studied the large, square wardrobe room. Stark lights hung from the ceiling on long wires. Below the lights, dozens of costumes were crammed onto rack after rack lined up one behind the other. The costumes hung on carefully marked hangers, categorized by style and period, male and female. It was like visiting a costume museum, Percy thought.

"Is it me," whispered Betty to Percy, as both followed the movements of Alice's bouncing waist-length hair, "or does her name suit her to a T?"

"I probably look just like a Persephone, myself, but maybe not." She thought of Ralph's comment about her name.

"Is that your given name, Persephone? Pretty. Mine's Elizabeth. I prefer it to Betty, but I'm too short to be an Elizabeth."

"I didn't know there was a height requirement for a name. If it's all the same to you, I'll call you Elizabeth from now on," remarked Percy, just as Alice approached them.

"You're here for the Second Witch costume?" Alice gave Percy a bored, sullen look.

"Yeah, I --"

"It's over here." Alice turned away and reached up for a many layered gunmetal gray and black gauze free-flowing garment from a rack. Blotches of a lighter gray dabbed here and there added to the overall grunginess.

Those long sleeves and train looked like double, double, toil and trouble for climbing up and down the platform stairs. Oy!

"Here's the hat." Alice threw the costume over one shoulder, dragging the bottom of it on the floor, while she sauntered over to another section of the room. Rows of canvas head blocks stood at attention on shelving, some still wearing hats or headgear used in the play. She reached up for a pointy black hat, the top of the cone bent to one side. Tattered clumps of grey fabric were sewed on in a haphazard pattern.

That's the ugliest hat I've ever seen, and I've seen some pretty ugly ones, like at Mother's church on Easter.

"What size shoe do you wear?" Alice looked at her from under heavy-lidded eyes.

"Eleven."

"We don't have any women's shoes that big. I'll have to give you a man's boot."

"How about if I wear my own? They're black and rubber soled. I like them."

Alice didn't answer, but shrugged and yawned.

"We keeping you up?" Percy's voice was light but had an edge to it. "Or you just hate your job?"

Alice shot her a startled look and became a little flustered. "Oh, I'm sorry. As a matter of fact, I haven't been sleeping all that well. The woman in the apartment next to mine has a new baby and the walls are paper thin. None of us are getting any sleep these days." She smiled and her face lit up.

"You should try smiling more often. You've got a good smile." Percy took the costume and hat from Alice. "I need to sign for these or something?"

"No, no, just bring them back after tonight's performance. You can keep them in your dressing room in between now and then." Alice moved away and toward a waiting actor.

Percy looked at Elizabeth. "I got a dressing room?"

"A hole in the wall with me and six other women, luv. We're hardly in it, anyway. We're onstage behind practically every scene, even the ones we don't have any lines in. We're there to represent the evil side of man."

"Do tell."

Elizabeth laughed. "Let's go to makeup. They'll draw and glue things on your face until you look like a monster out of a Lon Chaney movie."

"The glitter and glamour of show biz, huh?"

Chapter Twenty-seven

"Places, everyone!" The director's commanding voice from the front of the theatre house silenced cast and crew almost as one.

Percy stood on the platform trolley in front of the caldron waiting for the safety curtain of the proscenium arch to be raised. The sound of trumpets and battle music came over the loudspeakers. The trolley Percy stood on began to vibrate. She glanced over to the wing area, and two stagehands were pushing the three witches onstage with a long, wooden pole, stopping at stage left. Dim blue lights became brighter. Three blinding flashes of white hot lights overtook the stage, and then a deafening clap of thunder.

"What the hell was that?" Percy's shocked voice filled the silence. A stagehand tittered.

"Shhhh." Elizabeth smacked Percy on the butt, took a deep breath, and began to act in a voice 'projecting to the back of the house', as she called it.

"When shall we three meet again? In thunder, lightning, or in rain?"

There was silence. Elizabeth reached out her hand again, this time prodding Percy to speak.

"When the hurlyburly's done, When the battle's lost and won," the detective mumbled, the sound distorted to her by the large bulbous nose glued over her own.

"Louder." The director's voice cut through the dark beyond the footlights of the stage. "And project, for God's sake. Say it again."

"When the hurlyburly's done, When the battle's lost and won." Percy yelled out, her tone sounding nasal and flat. She coughed, unused to the strain it put on her throat.

Alfred, the Third Witch, spoke next. *"That will be ere the set of sun."* It could not have sounded more masculine or Brooklynese.

"Alfred," commanded Hugo Cranston. "Try it higher pitched and more British. You sound like you're at a Yankee baseball game. Do it again."

Alfred repeated the line. The delivery sounded exactly the same as the first time. There was a moment of silence.

"Where's my assistant? Where's my assistant?" Cranston screamed out to the universe.

The sound of thudding feet running down an aisle from the back of the theatre house to the front could be heard.

"Here I am, Mr. Cranston." A stuttering, youthful, female answered in the blackness of the unlit audience, her voice radiating eagerness and fear.

Another one of the possibilities, thought Percy. *A little young, but she could be the kid sister, Elsie.*

The cast and crew listened to the conversation taking place in the darkened and otherwise empty house.

"You find me two actresses to play the witches by tonight, the latest tomorrow," Cranston roared, even though the girl seemed to be standing close by.

"Yes, sir," came the meek reply.

"And I don't care if they fly in on their brooms from the moon. Is that clear?"

"Yes, sir."

"Go make the phone calls now, never mind following the light cues. Tell Equity we'll pay double. Just send us two actresses who know how to act."

"Yes sir."

And stop saying 'yes sir'."

"No, sir. I mean, yes, sir. I mean--"

"Just go," Cranston bellowed.

There was another sound of thudding feet, this time running from the front of the house to the back.

"Now then," crooned the director toward the stage in mock cordiality. "Let's start the ruddy play from the beginning, shall we? And let's try to do it in such a way that Shakespeare won't be spinning in his grave by curtain call." His voice rose with each word until it reached a crescendo at the end. "Lower the bloody curtain!"

In utter silence, a stagehand lowered the safety curtain.

* * * *

"There's not much to say about this acting business, is there?" Pop crept to Percy's side in the one instant neither of them were onstage.

"It has its drawbacks, Pop. You see that platform I stand on most of the time at the back of the stage? That's the spot I found Laverne." She pointed in the direction of the platform now pulled out of sightline from the audience.

"You mean the one in front of those backdrops that keep going up and down? I've never seen so much stuff flying up in the air only to come back down again ten minutes later."

"Keep your eye on the platform, Pop, and if anybody's up there not dressed as a witch, let me know. Someone's been practicing throwing a dagger from it to center stage, where the troupes fight their battles."

"I don't think I like that much, Persephone, especially as I'm one of the troupes."

"Intermission's coming soon. Let's talk during the break between Act One and Two. Sir Anthony is starting his 'If it were done when tis done' speech."

"He's pretty good. I don't know what he's saying half the time, but I believe he means it."

"I'm going up the platform soon. I have to wave my arms around and look menacing. I'm supposed to do the first half of the 'screw your courage to the sticking place' speech by myself, then the other two witches join me and we cackle together. I'd better go stand by. See you later."

Pop grabbed onto her arm and pulled her near. "I don't suppose you could keep that costume to take Oliver trick or treating in? I've never seen such an ugly getup."

"Not a chance, Pop." Percy moved to the back of the side stage, listening to the voices of the onstage actors playing Lord and Lady Macbeth. Though young for the part, the woman was good, Percy decided. You couldn't tell she was American.

'Prithee, peace:' Percy heard Macbeth say. *'I dare do all that may become a man; Who dares do more is none.'*

At her cue to move into place, Percy climbed the darkened steps, trying to maneuver the trailing sleeves and long train out of harm's way. She stood in place at the end of what she liked to call
the 'diving board'. While she waited to be pushed onstage, she practiced doing threatening gestures with her arms. Yards of material impeded her movements, no matter how hard she concentrated.

"Persephone, look out! Look out!!"

Her father's voice, loud and filled with alarm, broke into her reverie. Percy spun her body around and saw a mammoth archway, usually roped up and attached to the inside wall of the theatre by large hooks, coming at her like a wrecking ball. In that instant, she knew even dropping to the floor of the platform could not save her; it had to be removed from the area when this archway took its place.

With only the sparse lighting from the stage to guide her, Percy calculated the distance from the side of the platform to the hanging velvet curtains of the wings, three to four feet away. She sprang and tried to wrap her arms around the fabric to get some sort of hold to prevent her falling twenty feet to the floor below. Hampered by the yards of fabric clinging to her body as well as her body weight, she slid down a few feet before her hands got a solid grip. Her face buried in old, grimy velvet, she heard the crash of the heavy wooden archway as it struck the platform like a battering ram. Shattering the platform into smithereens, what was left of it careened onstage. The impact of both large objects caused a slight shudder in the area, causing her to momentarily lose her grip and drop down an inch or two more.

Everywhere around her, Percy heard the screaming of men and women, and then a ripping sound. Overhead, the old and worn material she was clinging to gave in to her weight and tore above her. She began to swing like Johnny Weissmuller in a Tarzan movie. Down, down she went, until she toppled to the floor, buried under yards of heavy cloth.

Chapter Twenty-eight

By the time Percy was uncovered from pounds of velvet, the show had come to a complete stop and the backstage lights were on. She felt hands pawing at the fabric, pulling and twisting it, often catching the sleeves and bodice of her witch's gown by mistake. Thoughts of suffocation overtook her until they were surpassed by anger. She fought her way to the top of the mound, and the first face she saw was Pop's.

"Persephone! My sweet child," he said, trying to embrace her.

"We don't have time for that, Pop, but thanks for the warning."

This encounter with yards of heavy, dusty fabric didn't help her headache, but she ripped off her putty nose and fake chin, threw them to the ground, and stood straight up. Her stance was unyielding. "Help me get out of this stupid costume, Pop, will you?"

Perplexed as to how to do it, he took hold of a drape in the sleeve and gave a tug. Elizabeth appeared from nowhere, attaching herself to Percy's other side.

"Percy! What happened? Are you all right? Let me help." She began trying to free the costume from the pile of velvet on the floor. Others stood by, unsure of what to do or even if they should try to help.

Kyle came running over to her as Percy tore out the neck of the garment, dropped it to the floor, and stepped out, dressed in her white blouse and black pants underneath.

"Are you okay?" He reached out to steady her, when she had a wobbly moment. She brushed him off.

"I'm fine. I'm just fine, although you have some cleaning up to do back here."

"Who is the person responsible for this?" Kyle yelled in his best stage manager's voice. "Where's the set crew?" His fingers snatched at a thick rope overhead still heaving in the dust laden air. "My God, look at that. It's been cut. Who did this? Who did this?"

"Never mind," Percy said, touching him on the arm to get his attention. "You won't find anyone taking responsibility for this." She turned to her father and Elizabeth, standing next to one another and whispered. "Pop, go get dressed and meet me in Wainwright's office. Elizabeth, take what's left of my costume back to wardrobe, change, and then you meet me in the office, too."

Cranston now arrived on the scene, coming from the audience to the back of the stage. He pushed his way through the small crowd.

"What the hell is going on around here? What happened now?" He looked at the damage done to the shattered archway and the platform beneath, reduced to rubble. "Lord love a duck. This is the end. This is the veritable end."

"Not quite," Percy said in a low voice. "But it *will* be ended and by me. Come on." She grabbed hold of the director's sleeve and pulled him along. She released her grip on him when she saw he trotted alongside her willingly, trying to keep up.

Without knocking, she barged into the producer's office. She opened her mouth to speak, but stopped when she saw the faces of Dexter Wainwright and Mavis as they turned to the sound of her entrance. Cranston, too, froze standing beside Percy, when he saw the two others.

Wainwright was seated, the receiver of the telephone still grasped in his hand, lying on the desk top. His face was ashen. Mavis stood behind him, one hand placed lightly on his shoulder, a tear running slowly down her cheek.

"What happened?" Percy closed the door after she and the director stepped inside.

"That was the police," Mavis said, in a barely audible voice. "Laverne is gone." She turned away, covering her face with her hands and sobbed into them.

"Poison," Dexter said in a dead tone. "Someone put poison into her intravenous tube. They have to do tests, but they think it might be rat poison." His face took on a puzzled, uncomprehending look. "How would anyone do that? Why would anyone do that?"

"Posing as a nurse or doctor, most likely," Percy replied. She didn't answer the second question, but reached over, took the phone from his hand, and replaced the receiver on the telephone base. "Do they have a time for this?"

"They said around eight-thirty this morning. What was that noise out there? Did something happen?" He looked from Cranston's face back to Percy.

This was a different man than Percy met only the day before. Wainwright seemed beaten down, unable to keep up with or comprehend anything.

"You could say that," Percy said. "That big archway stage left came down like a sledge hammer on the Weird Sisters platform. No one was hurt."

Mavis dropped her hands, took a sharp intake of breath, and spun around to stare at Percy.

"The police are coming at two o'clock to begin fingerprinting everyone in the theatre. Oh, my God," Wainwright said. It was his turn to bury his face in his hands. "I can't believe this, I can't believe this."

"Believe it," Percy said. "It will be better that way."

Cranston, who had stood quietly by, not uttering a sound, began spewing words. "Dex, we've got to close the show. And I want my money back. I gave you twenty thousand dollars in good faith, but we need to close the show, walk away from this, before anyone else gets killed. I want my money back," he said crossing the room and standing in front of the producer, nervous twitches charging through his body.

"I'm not returning your money," the producer said, coming to life. "There is no money to give back. It's all gone. I'm ruined, ruined."

Cranston grabbed the taller man's jacket collar in a threatening way. "Listen here, you son of a --"

Wainwright, in turn, took hold of the shorter man. They began to tussle in place, jockeying for the superior position, like two wrestlers in a ring.

Percy crouched down, stepped in between, and under the men's interlocked arms. She stood abruptly and brought her own arms up then down, breaking their grip on one another. She faced the director, the shorter man, and gave him a shove into a nearby chair.

"That's enough, both of you. You've been watching too many George Raft movies."

Wainwright pointed a shaky finger at Cranston. "He started it."

"Yeah, yeah. We're not in the school yard now, boys. Sit down, Wainwright. And shut up."

Wainwright ignored Percy and remained standing, glaring down at the director.

"Do what I'm telling you. Sit." She gave Wainwright a push. He plopped back into the chair at his desk.

"How can either of you behave like this?" Mavis fisted her hands and dropped them by her side, her body taut with emotion. She looked at both men with contempt on her face. "Laverne is dead. Carlisle is dead."

"And somebody tried to kill me just now," remarked Percy. "And if you don't mind my saying, I'm taking it personally."

"What?" Both men gaped at Percy, saying the word in unison. Mavis drew in a sharp breath.

Percy looked from director to producer. "You think that arch came down by itself? What are you, delusional?"

"We've got to close the show," Cranston repeated. "I'm going out there right now and dismissing the cast. Oh my God, my entire savings lost to you, you son of a --"

"I didn't tell you to invest with me! You begged me. Forty percent of a show for twenty thousand --"

Percy moved between the seated men that were precariously close to standing and getting into a skirmish again. "Shut up, both of you." She raised her voice above theirs. "I'm not telling you again. And make one move out of these chairs before I say so, I slap the two of you silly. You got that?" She glared first at the director, who nodded then to the producer, who leaned back in his chair and looked away.

"Well, I see this projecting your voice thing can get you somewhere. That and the threat of a knuckle sandwich." She turned to the director and spoke at a more normal level. "Cranston, tell me about your assistant."

"My assistant? Thelma?" Cranston appeared flummoxed.

"Who is she? What do you know about her? How long has she been with you?"

"Thelma?" Cranston stopped speaking and stared at Percy.

"Well, at least you know her name. Let's take it from there."

"My regular assistant joined the RAF last summer. When we came to the States, I couldn't find one decent man for the job. This bloody war," he muttered.

"Yeah, it seems to be interfering with a lot of people's lives," Percy said.

"I looked over the resumes of what was left." Cranston warmed to the subject. "And, frankly, I chose her because she was the cheapest. It comes out of my salary. I don't know one damned thing about her. Oh, yes. She studied drama at Cornell or some such place. She's good for bringing me coffee, not much else."

"Okay." Percy took a deep breath. "Here's what's going to happen, Mr. Illustrious Director. You're going to go out there and tell the cast and crew to take a two-hour break and come back at one-thirty to pick up where we left off with the run-through. And you're not going to mention anything about anybody being fingerprinted. I want the theatre cleared of everyone and all the doors locked, including the front of the house. Nobody stays but me."

"The stagehands have to clean up that mess," protested Cranston.

"I've seen them hustle when they have to. Tell them ten minutes and then out. You got me? Just make the announcement that the show will go on, no matter what."

Cranston stared at her in disbelief then let out a scoffing chuckle. "I'm not going to do any such thing. I --"

"Yes, you are. And you're going to give it the best acting job of your life." Percy moved closer to the seated, shaking man and put a hand on his shoulder. "Look Hugo, I want someone out there to think all they've done isn't working. The play needs to continue, at least for the moment."

"They'll just try again." Mavis's strangled voice came from a corner of the room.

"That's what I'm counting on," said Percy.

"The next time it will be me." The producer shuffled around in his chair, crossing one leg over the other. Then changing his mind, he uncrossed and re-crossed his legs repeatedly, his whole body vibrating with fear.

"No, not yet, Wainwright. Soon, but not yet. I got a feeling you haven't suffered enough. But by the looks of you, you're getting
there." She turned back to the director. "So stand up, Cranston. Get up, go out, and give them the Great White Way's version of Patrick Henry's speech. You know, Give me liberty or give me Broadway." He stared at her, unconvinced. "Do it right and you just might save your twenty grand."

He rose, straightened his shirt, smoothed his hair, and walked out without saying a word.

"I don't know what's happening. I can't keep up with any of this." Wainwright's eyes searched Percy's, as if for answers. "Do you have any idea what's going on around here?"

"I do. But I need to look in your files to make sure I'm right. Meanwhile, I want you to go out to lunch with Pop, who's going to keep an eye on you. Be back in an hour. You're picking up the tab, so bring a bunch of change."

"Out to lunch? I don't --"

"Just do it."

Wainwright didn't answer but nodded, chewing on a thumbnail.

"That's a bad habit, biting your nails. You should stop," Percy said.

There was a knock on the door. Pop opened it and stuck his head in. Through the open door, Percy could hear Cranston's voice in the background delivering a pompous, yet rousing speech about the traditions of the theatre.

"Pop, Elizabeth with you?"

"I'm right here." A contralto voice sounded on the other side of the door.

Percy went to the door and opened it wider. Both stepped inside. Percy closed the door behind them.

"Pop, you and Elizabeth are going to take Wainwright to the automat for lunch. Only eat or drink what comes out of the windows where you put the change in and nothing else. Sit in the middle of the restaurant and don't talk to anyone else. Use your key to get back in the theatre. Be sure the stage door is locked behind you. Got that?"

"Sounds good, Persephone," Pop said.

Elizabeth studied Percy. "Are you sure you're an assistant stage manager? You don't --"

"Yeah, yeah," Percy interrupted. "New breed and all that. Wainwright, wait outside the door with Elizabeth for a second. Pop will be right there. Remember, don't talk to anyone."

Wainwright got up and wordlessly followed Elizabeth out. They both waited just outside the office door. Speech over, Cranston was receiving a hip, hip hurrah from the cast and crew, spattered with light applause.

Percy leaned into her father's ear. "Pop, you got the Mauser in the glove compartment of Ophelia?"

"Yes. The car's right outside."

"Bring it in with you when you come back."

Pop's eyebrows, now devoid of the fake black hairs, shot up. "You expecting trouble, Persephone?"

"'Be prepared', as Oliver's cub scout leader says." Percy smiled. "Go on now, have a good lunch. I've got some files to read. See you in an hour."

"Be careful, child."

"Always."

Chapter Twenty-nine

Evelyn, I put the rat poison in the I.V. bag like you said to do, but things keep going wrong. I almost got caught at the hospital. One of the doctors thought I was a real nurse and told me to come with him into surgery. I ran away, but I know they'll tell the police. What are we going to do? It's that fat woman's fault. She's snooping into everything. Stop her!

Elsie

Chapter Thirty

Percy shut the office door and turned around. Mavis was still standing in the corner of the room.

"Would you really have slapped them silly? I'd like to have seen that." Mavis's tone held a forced delight, her eyes belying the wariness beneath. She stood rigidly in place, not moving.

"Wainwright is a coward and Cranston is a good five inches shorter than me. I say or do whatever gets me results. But let's talk about you."

Percy focused her attention on Mavis. In response, the girl crossed her arms over her chest in defiance.

"You're a complicated kid, Mavis, but before you leave this room, you're going to tell me who you really are and what you're doing here. It'll be easier for everybody." She went to the desk and picked up the receiver of the phone, keeping an eye on the younger woman. Mavis dropped her defensive stature and looked away.

"You think about it, kiddo, while I make this call. People are getting killed right and left. There's no place for secrets at this point. And yes, you can stay in the room while I telephone. Sit down over there." Percy pointed to the chair Cranston had vacated.

Mavis crossed over to the chair and dropped into it. Percy dialed a number, hiked one leg over the corner of the desk, and sat down.

"Hello, Mother? I'm just calling to see how everything is." She pulled the bag of pistachios out of her pocket, but kept her eye on Mavis while she spoke. "No kidding. Well, that is good news. You tell Sylvia I'm glad they located him." She listened, while she popped a pistachio in her mouth. "Yes, that is too bad about his hand, but I'll bet Sylvia's glad he's alive, even with only one." She paused and listened. "Yes, Mother, 'Where there's life, there's hope'. Is Freddy still there with Oliver?" She listened again. "Good, good. He's a good kid. Tell Oliver I'll see him tonight and I'm
looking forward to taking him trick or treating tomorrow. No, the headache's a little better. The aspirin helped. See you later."

Percy hung up the phone, and turned back to the private secretary. "Come to a decision?" She could see the girl's internal struggle. "Come on, I know most of it, anyway." It was part lie, part truth, but Percy went with it. She dropped nut shells in an ashtray on the desk and looked at Mavis.

"You know who I really am?"

Percy nodded.

"How?"

"About two years ago I saw a picture of you in a magazine. You were half hidden behind your father's back at premier of a movie. But there was enough of you peeking out to be recognizable. It took me a while to place you, but I never forget a face."

"You read movie magazines?" Mavis almost sounded amused.

"I don't but my kid sister, Sera, does. She wanted our mother to make her a copy of the gown the starlet standing next to your father was wearing. Mother's a good seamstress."

"Just my luck. It's the only time I ever had my photo taken with him in public." Mavis sounded mildly perturbed. "So you know my father is J.D. Mayer, one of the three men who started Colossal Pictures." She came forward on the edge of her seat, proud and excited. "Look, Father said if I made my own way in show business for one year, he'd produce my picture. I've written a screenplay and it's a knock-out, too."

"I'll bet." Percy popped another pistachio in her mouth and extracted the shell, as the girl went on.

"But Father wouldn't hear of me writing or producing a movie because I'm a girl. Only because I'm a girl! I have to prove myself. Can you believe that?"

"I can."

"If I was his son, he would have backed me in an instant. Life's so unfair."

"Yeah, I just heard about a man who lost his hand in the service of his country, and he was lucky, at that. For awhile, everyone thought he was dead. So what are you doing here and incognito?"

"I thought if I applied for the job as Dexter Wainwright's secretary, I could learn about the theatre. That would give me
credibility back in Hollywood. And I've learned a lot. I didn't tell Dexter who I was, because…because…"

"Wainwright would probably hit your father up for some money, him being the kind of chump that he is."

Mavis let out a nervous giggle and nodded. "That would have destroyed everything." She looked up into Percy's face, her clear, brown eyes solemn with intent. "Please, Percy, if you tell Dexter it will ruin everything. He'll contact my father, ask him for money, if not for this show, for the next, and Father will have a fit. Also, I want to do it on my own. No favoritism."

"I'll see what I can do." Percy rose from the desk. "But no promises. Meanwhile, I have to go through the files on everyone connected with this turkey, including you. Did you lie when you filled out the job application?" Mavis looked down in embarrassment. "I thought so. It's easy enough to do.

Nobody checks on anything. Someday they will, but for now you have to read between the lines." Percy let out a sigh. "Makes my job harder, but what are you going to do? Hand the files over and I'll get started."

Chapter Thirty-one

The sound of a baby's cry broke Percy's concentration. Mavis had gone to lunch a short time before, promising to bring Percy back a Nathan's hotdog. The girl had left the office door ajar, as requested. Percy wanted to hear what, if anything, was going on in the rest of the theatre. Other than the creaks and occasional bang of ancient pipes, the theatre had been quiet. Giving the files a quick once over; the thinking part was still in progress when she heard the cry again.

Percy leapt up, wondering what the hell a baby was doing in a locked theatre, and stepped into the hallway. Looking toward the stage, she saw a small animal scurry across stage. Sir Anthony's cat.

I thought he never left the dressing room! This is not good.

She hurried into the wings and called out to the feline. "Kitty, kitty, kitty. Here, kitty, kitty, kitty." The cat paused and turned around, looking at her. Percy crouched down and called again. The cat hesitated for a moment then darted back across the stage to her. She picked him up and looked around. No signs of anyone. The plaintive cry came again from the animal, loud and insistent, but ending with a purr. She clutched him to her bosom and stroked the silky fur.

"Let's go find your owner." Percy was filled with a certain amount of apprehension.

She headed to the back of the backstage area and over to the star's dressing room. The door was ajar. Percy pushed at it with her foot and it opened wide on creaky hinges.

Sir Anthony lay on the sofa on his back, one arm over his chest, the other to the floor. The cat began to struggle. Percy shut the door behind her, set the cat down, and crossed over to the man. Was he sleeping or was he dead?

Around this theatre, it could be either.

She touched the side of his neck. Warm. There was a pulse. Percy leaned in, about to shake the actor, when he awoke with a start. He cried out at seeing someone leaning over him.

"What the bloody hell? What are you doing in my room?" He sat up and pushed away from her.

Percy went to the other side of the coffee table, hands on her hips. "Here's one for you. What the bloody hell are you doing in the theatre? It was supposed to have been cleared of everyone."

"Oh, pshaw," he said dismissively. "Rules like that don't apply to me." He ran fingers through his unkempt hair and stretched. "What are you doing here, my fiery Persephone?"

"I'm returning your cat. I found him wandering around on the stage."

"Impossible. He never strays beyond that door. I keep him inside, always."

"Nevertheless, your lordship," Percy's tone was mocking. "I found him on the stage and the door to this room was open."

"Again, I say impossible. I closed that door, myself."

"Say what you like." Percy continuing to watch the seated actor, now crossed her arms over her chest. She turned her attention to the coffee table that stood between the two of them. "You drinking again?" She pointed to a whiskey bottle standing at the end of the table.

"Certainly not. I was sleeping. I haven't been getting much sleep, what with what's been…going on." He picked up the bottle. "Where did that come from? Old Bushmills, my favorite. A gift from one of my many admirers, I assume." He glanced up at her and winked. "Or did you bring this to me, you little vixen?"

"Not only didn't I bring it, I wouldn't drink it if I was you. The bottle is full and yet the seal has been broken."

"That doesn't mean...what does that mean?" He looked up at her questioningly.

"Around here it could mean anything. Where did the bottle come from? Why is the seal broken? Who left the door open? If I were you, I'd pour that booze out in the sink over there."

"And waste a fifteen dollar bottle of good whiskey? I don't think I can do that." He caressed the bottle lovingly.

She picked up a nearby hand towel. "On second thought, it should be analyzed, maybe tested for fingerprints." She tried to take the bottle from his hands with it.

"No! I'm going to drink it. Give it here."

They tussled for ownership of the bottle for a split second and it crashed to the floor, breaking into smithereens.

"Well, there goes a couple of possible clues." Percy looked down at the broken glass.

"Now look what you've done." Sir Anthony glared at her. "Throw a towel over that so Anny doesn't step on any glass." Dejected, he held his head in his hands staring down at the floor. The cat jumped up and lay beside him on the sofa.

"Yes, your majesty." Percy threw the towel she had in her hand over the wet mess on the floor then sat down in the chair near him. "Time to talk."

Sir Anthony sneered at her. "I know about you. You're not an assistant stage manager. You're a female detective, hired by that prick producer to lay every wicked deed at my feet."

"How did you find out?"

"Hugo Cranston told me. He was, as you Yanks say, on a fishing expedition.

As is often the case, he told me more than he bloody well learned."

"Just so you know, I'm not here to lay anything at your feet, wicked or otherwise. Unless you did it." She leaned forward, looking deeply into the actor's bloodshot eyes. "You making all this trouble around here? Truth time."

He stared back at her openly then shook his head.

"You'll pardon me if I don't quite believe you. You're one helluva an actor."

He looked down at his folded hands and shook his head again. "I don't think I could fool you, you being Zeus's daughter." He threw her a weak smile. "I know I started this, with the pranks and all. I thought it was just a game I was playing, trying to get my own back at Dex for stealing my show. Anytime I was off-stage, which was not often, I'd run to the hidden microphone and make groans and moans into it. It was a lark. Then one day, I was giving my 'If it were done' speech and the sounds started in on me. Then the sandbag fell right where I'd been standing not ten seconds before. I could have been killed."

"Did you get a threatening letter?"

"You know about that?" His reply was startled.

"I suspected. Let me see it." Percy extended her hand.

"I don't have it. I tore it up and threw it away."

"What did it say? What did it look like?"

"Cut out letters glued to a piece of paper. Something about I would die if I stayed around or some such thing. I can't remember. I threw it out immediately."

"Did you tell anyone about it?"

"No. I thought it was Mr. Prick trying to scare me off. I wouldn't give him the satisfaction. But things kept escalating and then Carlisle dying like that. That was my fault. If I hadn't sent him up there..." Sir Anthony looked down again at his hands. "I'm done with this business." He said let out a long, dramatic sigh. "If I could leave this theatre and never come back, I would do it. Become a plumber, a doctor, anything but an actor."

"I doubt that," Percy replied, with a gentle smile.

"I don't want anyone hurting my cat. You know, to get at me." The actor picked up the feline and set it in his lap, stroking it lovingly. "Anny means everything to me. He's the only family I have."

"What does that make your wife, chopped liver?"

"Who? Linda? Linda and I...that was a mistake. I was trying to get one better of Dex. You know, marry his ex. Dex screwed around with my first wife, so it was only fair. Dex and I have been jousting one another since way back when. To be fair, he warned me Linda was an expensive bitch, but I didn't believe him. Too bad."

"Uh-huh. Maybe you should leave the cat at the hotel for awhile. Just until this is over."

He didn't respond but nodded, kissing the cat on the head.

"Okay." Percy rose. "I got places to go, people to see, things to do." She crossed to the door. "This has a deadbolt on it. Use it when you're in here." Her eye caught another door in the side wall, painted the same color white, and almost blending into the wall.

"That door's the closet." She pointed to the opposite wall. "And that one's the john. Where does the third door go?"

"Oh, yes." A guilty expression crossed Sir Anthony's face. "That connects to the dressing room of my co-star, Lady Macbeth. It used to be Felicity's and now belongs to Cynthia. Lovely girl."

Percy went to the door and tried it. It opened on well-oiled hinges. Stepping into the actress's room, there was the smell of greasepaint and a strong, sweet perfume. Percy tested the knob on the hall door of the dressing room. It opened. She turned back to Sir Anthony. Carrying the cat, he had followed her into the room.

"I thought all the dressing room doors were supposed to be kept locked when no one was inside. When the actor is leaving, he or she is supposed to return the key to Ned."

The actor shrugged, stroking his pet. "The best laid plans of mice and men, my dear."

"Does the connecting door have a lock on your side?" Percy walked past the actor and back into his dressing room. He followed.

"Not that I know of. I haven't seen one. I never thought of anyone coming in that way."

Percy picked up a small wooden chair with a high back and crammed it under the door knob. She tried pulling the door open several times but it stayed firmly in place.

"You're scaring me, fiery Persephone," Sir Anthony said, after watching her for a spell. "Why all these precautions?"

"Let's just say I like the way you do the 'I dare do all that may become a man; Who dares do more is none' speech. You've got a knack with words."

"Why, you care, my sweet girl." He advanced toward her.

"Just lock the door and keep your pants on. You never know when you'll have to make a hasty exit." She turned to leave his dressing room.

"One more thing, oh daughter of Zeus," Sir Anthony called after her. "You *do* know Wainwright has the production insured for a hundred and fifty thousand dollars. If anything happens of a catastrophic nature and this show comes to a grinding halt, he gets that lovely bundle of money."

Percy stopped in her tracks and turned around, then walked back to the actor standing in the doorway. "I thought if something happened and the production didn't get mounted, it would revert back to you."

"That's only if I'm still alive, dear girl, only if I'm still alive."

"You know he sold Cranston forty percent of the show." Percy watched the actor closely. "Why would he do that if he was trying to close it?"

"Did he?" The actor's answer was smooth. "I couldn't say. You must ask him."

"Is that standard? An insurance policy like that? How'd you find out?"

"It's been done." The actor transferred the purring cat from
his arms to one shoulder. He held it like a child. "But could he collect? That's another thing."

"Why wouldn't he be able to collect? This is a fascinating discussion, Sir Anthony. You seem to know a lot more than you've been spilling."

"In answer to your question about how I know, the man *told* me. It was his way of warning me off, to try to make me to stop disrupting the production. But if it's proven he incapacitated his own production, then, of course he couldn't collect, could he?" He rubbed the cat's neck.

"So which way is it? In your considered opinion," Percy challenged. "And enough with the cat, already. Put him down and talk to me."

With gentle hands, Sir Anthony removed the cat from his shoulder, dropped it to the floor of his dressing room, and closed the door. Leaning against it, he turned back to Percy, with a more serious expression on his face.

"You mean, is there really an insurance policy? I can't say I've seen the documents, but I wouldn't put anything past that prick. Over-insure a production then sabotage it to prevent it from opening, sounds a lot like the Dexter Wainwright I've come to know and despise."

"So you say. Or is this feud on the up and up? Possibly you're in this together. You *both* sabotage the production, each sending up a smoke screen for the other. In the end, he gets the one-hundred and fifty grand and you get your production back. Almost a win-win situation for everyone except the dead."

"Why, Persephone, what fire in your eyes as you say that. One would almost believe you thought me capable of such dastardly deeds."

They stood for a moment in a face-off, Sir Anthony wearing a smirk and Persephone with a cool detachment. She was the first to break off.

"I'm beginning to see that you are in every way Dexter Wainwright's equal. And I do not mean that as a compliment, your nibs." She turned on her heel and strode away.

"You've hurt me to the quick, oh fiery goddess," he called after her.

I'll hurt you someplace else, if you push me too far, Percy thought, but kept walking back to the office.

Chapter Thirty-two

She slammed the office door behind her, the sound reverberating in the silent theatre.

Control yourself, Percy. Maybe that's what he wants, to throw you off your game. Everybody's got an angle.

She rubbed her forehead, the ache inside her head increasing with her annoyance. Reaching inside her pocket, she pulled out a small bottle of aspirin and downed two, swallowing them with the tepid tea.

This damned headache. I can't let it interfere with my thinking. Where was I? Oh, yeah. If his nibs is to be believed, Wainwright has kept something from you once again, and it ain't something small. I'm going to punch that son of a bitch in the nose one of these days, just to hear it break. Stop, Percy. Leave that delicious thought for later. Okay, take a deep breath.

She did and felt better. Was the aspirin working so fast? Probably not. Sometimes just the idea of something helps.

Why would Wainwright hire you if he was doing this to himself? To give him more credibility, of course. If the insurance company contested payment, he could say he even brought in a private detective to find the culprits. That means if you don't solve this, your career might be over before it starts.

Okay, so after that dandy thought, what do you know; what are the facts? Two people have died, four if you count the ones from the uptown fire two weeks ago. Someone sent threatening letters, maybe to even more people than have stepped up to the plate. There could be a lot more. In fact, maybe every cast member got one. If I don't get a break soon, I'll talk to the remaining actors and see what I can learn.

Next, Felicity Dowell. If she is to be believed, someone tried to poison her then run her down with a truck. Maybe true, maybe not. Maybe she's taking advantage of what's been going on around here. It could be a ploy on her part to get out of her contract and into working with Lawrence Oliver. I can see it. He's a little on the short side, but he can put his shoes under my bed anytime.

Don't get off the track, Percy. Keep your Libido in check. Aspirin working. Good.

Okay. For the moment, let's say I believe all these things happened exactly the way people say they did. That means this has been well-planned, far-reaching, and gone on for awhile. Done by one person, it would be tough. If it is Wainwright, he had to have had help. He doesn't strike me as a guy that likes to get his hands dirty.

But who? Could be his new partner, Hugo Cranston. Forty percent of a hundred and fifty grand is not a bad return on twenty thousand bucks. Or another candidate is his seemingly mortal enemy, Sir Cat Lover. This feud thing could be an act to throw us off. All three have access to everything in the theatre, any time, night or day. Huge buckos is usually the number one motive.

But if it ain't the bucks, then there are the two daughters of Jacob Cohen. Vendetta with a capitol 'V'. From what I know, they have plenty of reason to want to do more than punch Wainwright in the nose. If they're in the theatre, they too, have access to just about everything.

Motive and access. It comes down to that either way. So, Persala, as Mrs. Goldstein would say, don't let anyone throw you off with their emotional claptrap.

A knock on the door interrupted her wrangled thoughts.

"Come on in."

Percy was glad of the interruption and looked toward the door. Wainwright, Pop, and Elizabeth walked inside.

"You can see he's safe and sound," Pop indicated the producer. "Here's what you asked for from the glove compartment of the car." Wrapped in a white towel, he handed her the German Mauser pistol brought back by her uncle as a souvenir of World War One. "You be careful now." Pop's tone was pointed.

"I don't mean to be rude," said Wainwright, in a churlish tone, "but I need to use the Gents. Am I allowed to go to the john?"

"Not alone," Percy replied. "Pop, you want to go with him?"

"Come on, fellow." Pop moved toward the door. "We'll be right back, ladies."

Percy nodded, setting the towel and its holding on the table beside her.

"Elizabeth." Percy turned to the petite actress hovering in the doorway. "Come on inside. I'd like your help with a few things."

"Me?" Elizabeth looked flustered. "What could you possibly want with me? Don't I have to get ready for the run-through?"

"Not yet. Nobody else is back. Sit down." She gestured to the chair opposite her in the small room. "I've been going through the files, Elizabeth, and I see that you're listed as Elizabeth Henning, a woman who was raised in an orphanage in Glasgow. That's in Scotland."

"I..I..." Elizabeth stuttered and then stopped.

"You told me you were born in East London and that your 'mum' said to take refuge where you could get it. We have a few discrepancies here."

Elizabeth never looked into the older woman's eyes, but licked her lips several times, saying nothing.

"I want to see your passport. I know you have one. You can't get into this country without it. You're going to have to show it to the cops soon enough, anyway, unless I can solve this. Tell me the truth. Maybe I can help you."

"No, no, why? I ain't done nothing. They can't...I can't...Oh, sweet Jesus." She grabbed Percy's hand in hers, tears spilling from her eyes.

"Please don't let them send me back to England. I hate it there. It's ever so much nicer here."

"Who's passport is it, Elizabeth? Or is that even your name?"

Elizabeth dropped Percy's hand and threw herself back in the chair. When she spoke her voice sounded tired and far away.

"Elizabeth is my true name, but nothing else." She shivered, as if suddenly cold, and closed her eyes. "It was right after the Blitz. There were so many bombs. They kept falling for hours. I'll never forget it; the falling bombs, the explosions, the people screaming." She cupped her hands over her ears, as if trying to block out the sounds. After a moment, she went on in a monotone.

"Mum and me, we ran to a shelter in the middle of the night. When we come back the next morning, the whole block was gone. I couldn't even tell where our flat had been. Mum got taken in by
some rich old bitty she worked for. She could sleep in a little room off the kitchen, the larder. There wasn't room for me. That night I went back to dig through the rubble, trying to find my best shoes. That's when I seen her purse with this passport in it, didn't I? Elizabeth "Betty" Henning from Glasgow; same first name as me. Not much older. And she looked like me, too, at least, on her passport. I never saw her... alive." Elizabeth gulped after the admission.

"Her hand was sticking up from under some bricks about three feet away from where I was digging. Looked right eerie in the moonlight. But I dug for her 'til me own hands were bleeding, trying to save her. She were as dead as you can be. There was some money and a third class ticket on the Oceana in the purse. I found her journal, too, saying she'd saved up enough money to go to New York. She wanted to be an actress, you see. She don't have no next of kin, said so right there on the passport. If anyone asked, I was going to tell them I was sent to London after I was born. Nobody asked." She shrugged. "So I took over her life; mine were so bloody awful. I tried to do a Scottish accent in the beginning, but I ain't much of an actress."

"I think you're pretty good, Elizabeth, when you concentrate." Percy smiled at her.

"I'm a damn sight better than you," Elizabeth said, wiping her eyes and returning Percy's smile. "You going to squeal on me?"

"No." Percy paused. "Elizabeth, living a lie is tougher than you think, but I'll keep your secret for you."

Elizabeth thought about it then nodded. "I wouldn't a done it if we didn't have the same first name. It seemed like fate. "You know, 'what's in a name?' What's the rest of that quote? Romeo and Juliet, innit?"

Percy smiled. "Actually, the meaning is just the opposite. 'What's in a name? That which we call a rose by any other name would smell —'" Percy broke off speaking and slowly rose from the chair, her face showing a sudden comprehension. "I have been so stupid. Of course."

The office door banged opened and Pop staggered in holding his head. Wainwright was nowhere in sight.

Chapter Thirty-three

Elsie, it's now or never. Everything we've been working for might come to a crashing halt thanks to that fat woman detective. At first, I didn't think you were right about her but now I see. She's not as stupid as she looks. We need to stop her then do what we planned from the beginning. The cabinet was locked, but I broke the glass. The two daggers are mine. Meet me in the secret place, but be careful. This is for father and mamma and all that was ours. Now is the time.

Evelyn

Chapter Thirty-four

"Pop! What happened?" Percy jumped up and ran to her father, who was leaning against the door frame for support.

"Are you all right?" Elizabeth stood and took a step toward him.

"I'm all right. I don't know what happened," he mumbled. "Somebody snuck up behind me and hit me on the head in the men's room. I was standing there talking to Wainwright and --"

"Where is he, Pop?" Percy stepped out in the hallway, looking both ways.

"I thought maybe he was back here. I was only out for a minute or two."

"You better sit down, Pop, while I go look for him." Percy picked up the white towel and unwrapped the Mauser." Elizabeth let out a gasp when she saw the gun. "Elizabeth, lock the door behind me and call the cops. Tell them to get down here right away. Take care of Pop, too."

"No siree bob. I'm going with you." Pop shook his head, as if to clear it, and stepped out the door, heading back to where he came from.

"Just a second," Percy called out. She ran to Ned's hole in the wall then checked the back stage entrance of the theatre, as well. She came back to her father's side. "Ned's not there and the door is locked. Whoever else is in here has a key. We don't know where they are."

They both stood motionless for a moment assessing their surroundings. The theatre was still. Only the work lights illuminated necessary areas, such as stairs and pathways. Other parts of the theatre seemed recessed, mysterious in their gloom. It was the perfect place for all types of chicanery to happen.

"Whatever we're going to do, Persephone, we need to do it quietly. I don't like this." Pop's voice was barely a whisper.

"Me neither." Percy answered in kind. "Did you check the bathroom stalls before you came back to the office, just in case?"

Pop nodded.

Before Percy could say more, they heard a noise overhead, maybe a cry, mixed in with the echoes and creaks of the old theatre. A smattering of dust rained down on upstage center, directly under where the catwalk soared above.

Father and daughter looked up and then back at each other.

"I'll climb up this set of rungs, Pop." Still whispering, Percy pointed to the rungs a few feet away. "You take those on the other side of the stage. Be careful, Pop. Be quick but as quiet as you can be. Maybe we can surprise whoever's up there."

Pop nodded. "That's why I always wear rubber-soled shoes, just like I taught you. Be careful with that weapon, child." He gestured to the pistol in her hand. "I don't care if you are a better shot than me."

"Safety's on, Pop."

He nodded again before taking off on silent feet and dashing across the stage.

Percy tucked the Mauser in the waistband at the back of her pants and began her climb. At one point, not even half way up, her hands became so sweaty, her fingers started to slip on the metal. She paused for a second, wrapped one arm around the inside of the rungs, while she wiped her hand off on her pants then repeated the process with the other hand. Starting the climb again, she had a serious talk with herself.

Calm down, Percy. Think about Oliver and taking him trick or treating. And you need to get him a stuffed parrot. These are the important things. And not getting killed. Concentrate on not getting killed.

At the top of the ladder, Percy swung her foot over to the catwalk and turned on her flashlight. In its sharp beam of light, she caught two men and a woman in a dramatic scene at the heart of the walk. The tall man in the middle was leaning backward over the low railing, near the point of toppling over the side, as he tried to get away from a dagger at his throat.

"Evelyn!" Percy called out to the stage manager, in a loud and authoritative voice. "I know who you are. Your name is Evelyn Cohen, not Kyle. And you're the son of Jacob Cohen. In England,
Evelyn is not an uncommon first name for a boy. Next to you is your sister, Elsie, not your girlfriend. Everything is out in the open, Evelyn. It's over."

The stage manager turned around at the sound of her voice, waving the dagger, the steel glinting in the light of Percy's torch. The producer dropped down to the floor of the catwalk. Sobbing, he covered his head with his arms in a protective manner.

"I admit it." Percy moved closer. "You had me going with your first name. I thought I was looking for the two daughters of Jacob Cohen, instead of a brother and sister."

On the other side of him, Elsie aka Alice, continued to wield her dagger, but in a less aggressive manner. She took her attention off Wainwright and looked at Percy.

"Go away," the assistant wardrobe mistress cried. "Leave us alone."

"Can't do that, Elsie." Percy continued to walk slowly toward them. "You've been a bad girl." She focused on the stage manager. "And he's been a bad boy. Evelyn, throw the dagger down. It's no use. Like I said, I know everything."

"You know nothing," Evelyn said, spittle spraying from his mouth. Even from this distance, his frenzied agitation and the intensity of his anger seemed to pump through him like an electrical charge.

"Yes, I was his son and heir. I was set to inherit everything until him." Evelyn pointed with the dagger to the crouching producer. Evelyn began to sob. "He poisoned our father. And because of him, our precious mamma jumped to her death. Now he's going to jump to his. He destroyed our family. We lost everything." The sobs turned to screams of rage. "He has to die. So you back off, lady."

"Please help me," Wainwright whimpered, catching Evelyn's attention once more.

"You! You need to die!" He wheeled back to the producer and drew back the hand with the dagger in it, preparing to strike.

Percy dropped the flashlight, sprang the ten feet or so forward, and grabbed Evelyn's arm on its forward thrust. Within inches of the producer's hunched-over back, Percy fought to break the young man's hold on the dagger. The thrashing about caused the catwalk to vibrate, making it hard for sure footing. Wainwright threw his arms over his head, but did nothing else to protect himself.

As Percy grappled with the stage manager, she thought, *Can this catwalk hold four people at one time? Scratch that. Five. Pop should be on the other side near Elsie by now.*

Evelyn broke free of her grip, pivoted, and kicked her in the stomach. She fell back on the grating, her hand landing on the small flashlight. Grabbing it, she leapt up again, and faced her assailant.

"I see it's time to take care of you, you fat bitch," said Evelyn, advancing on her in the shadows. He waved the dagger menacingly.

"That's *Miss* fat bitch to you, buster. And let's see who takes care of who," replied Percy, pulling the Mauser out from behind her with her free hand. She pointed the light on the pistol and then at the stage manager. He momentarily froze.

Sounds of a struggle on the other side of the catwalk diverted Percy's attention. The catwalk went from vibration to shuddering, throwing everyone off-balance. Percy assumed a wide stance, and focused on the stage manager, who looked more insane with each passing heartbeat.

"I've got the girl," Pop yelled from the other side of the walk.

The shuffling became noisier, momentarily distracting Percy and Evelyn, but not Wainwright. The producer leapt up and pushed at Evelyn in his effort to get by. The movements of the catwalk became even more intense with his pounding footsteps. He ran to the end of the catwalk and practically jumped onto the rungs, heading down.

Percy turned her attention back to the fight on the far end, involving her father and Elsie, and made a move in that direction. Just as Percy was about to call out, she heard a yelp from her father and the sound of a body falling over the rail, coupled with a short cry.

"Pop! Pop," Percy shouted. The push of Pop's falling body caused the catwalk to gyrate up and down, as well as side to side. She heard a metallic screeching but ignored it, screaming for her father.

Evelyn lunged at her with the dagger. Percy swung at his face with the butt of her gun and connected, not once but twice. He fell to the grating and lay still. Percy aimed the Mauser in the direction she'd last seen Elsie, but the girl seemed to have vanished. Had she fallen, too? No, no. it was just one person. Pop.

Oh, my God! Pop!

Percy snatched the dagger from the grating and hurried to the spot from where she heard her father fall. It was hard to move quickly on the vibrating catwalk and she continued to scream his name every step of the way. Panic filled her being as never before.

"Persephone," came her father's faint cry from somewhere below the catwalk, interrupting her horrifying thoughts.

"Pop, Pop!" Hope surged within her. "Where are you?"

"I'm here. I fell on the wooden horse. I think I broke my leg." His voice filled with pain, he let out a groan.

Percy leaned over as far as she dared, searching with her flashlight. Fifteen feet down her father straddled the life-size, inanimate beast, his arms wrapped around the neck. One of Pop's legs was in an awkward position.

"Hang on, Pop. I'll get you down!"

As she made a move for the side of the catwalk, a stagehand's voice shouted up, "What the hell is going on up there? Get off my catwalk. It ain't safe."

"You," Percy bellowed back. "Lower the ropes for the wooden horse, but do it carefully. There's an injured man hanging on it."

"What?" The voice from below was filled with incredulity. "What the hell is --?"

"Just do it!" Percy screamed. "And be careful. Pop's hurt."

"Okay, okay."

After a moment's silence, the screeching sound of rarely used winches being turned reverberated throughout the theatre.

"Hang on, Pop," Percy shouted. "You'll be down in no time."

"I'm hanging."

Keeping one eye on the unmoving Evelyn, Percy watched her father being lowered until he disappeared from her sight into the darkness below.

"You still there, Pop?" Percy yelled. "What's going on?"

"I got him." The stagehand's voice rose from the darkness beneath. "I'm getting him off the horse now."

Shortly after, there was the murmur of voices. She caught a word or two, enough to know Pop was safe. The faint sounds of police sirens wafted up to her.

"Call an ambulance for Pop then throw on all the lights in the joint," Percy ordered. "Especially if you got some up here."

"Okay, okay. One thing at a time. Don't have any lights up there. Nobody's supposed to be up there but me," the stagehand grumbled.

Breathing a huge sigh of relief, Percy went back to Evelyn Cohen, and prodded him with the toe of her shoe. She shone her light on his inert body. His face was bloodied from the butt of her gun, swelling near the jaw line. Satisfied he was still unconscious; she put the safety back on and returned the pistol to her waistband. She threw the dagger at the back brick wall, where she knew no one was and nothing would be damaged, except possibly the wretched weapon.

It struck the far bricks with a clatter and fell to the depths below, landing with a small clink. The sirens became louder. More than one police car approached.

The police will be here any minute. I'll have to tell them Elsie is still on the loose, armed, and possibly dangerous.

Percy removed the leather belt from around her waist and knelt down. "There's a few good things to being fat," she said aloud, as she pulled Evelyn's arms behind him. "I carry plenty of restraining material right on me." Percy wrapped the belt around his hands, put one end through the buckle, and pulled. Feeling it was tight enough, she tied the thin leather into a tight knot. She pushed his body so his arms were against the railing and wove the remainder of the belt in and out of the meshing, once again, pulling it tight. She double-knotted the belt.

That should hold him if he wakes up before the cops get here.

Below her a flood of lights came on, dimly illuminating even where she was. Percy stood and looked around her, realizing for the first time her headache was gone.

Good to know a combination of aspirin and an adrenalin rush will get rid of a headache, but I don't need another day like this.

The catwalk had calmed down and was easier to traverse. She headed for the opposite side of the theatre, keeping an eye out for Elsie. The girl was nowhere to be seen but that didn't mean she wasn't around, ready to pounce with the other dagger.

If I never see a dagger again in my life, it'll be too soon for me.

As she got to the rungs, prepared to go down to the stage level, she noticed the hidden, short door to the storeroom ajar.

What have we here?

Wanting to get to her father's side as quickly as possible, Percy was tempered with the knowledge that if Elsie was hiding inside the storeroom, the girl could be dangerous. Thoughts of the kerosene-filled lamp came to Percy's mind.

I wouldn't put it past her to start a fire and try to burn the theatre down with us in it.

She removed the Mauser from her waistband, checked the magazine clip, and released the manual safety again. Crouching down with the pistol in one hand and the flashlight in the other, Percy pushed the door open and crawled inside.

The second dagger lay on the floor glittering like a piece of jewelry in the beam of her light. On the alert, Percy took a moment to pick it up and shove it in her pocket.

In the death-like quiet, Percy moved the flashlight methodically from place to place. Somewhat familiar with the room, she was no longer taken aback when she saw the intimidating Statue of Liberty glaring down at her. The light finally rested on Elsie sitting on the floor in a corner. Back against the wall, the girl had her arms wrapped around her drawn up legs, head resting on her knees. Her Alice in Wonderland hair cascaded down to the floor, making the whole scenario macabre and surreal. On the inside of one of the girl's calves was an angry, infected gash, a drooping sock no longer shielding it from sight.

"You should put Mercurochrome on that scratch," Percy said, standing and aiming the Mauser at her.

Elsie slowly raised her head and tried to look past the beam of light shining in her face. "Is he dead? Did you kill my brother?" Her British accent returned in this unguarded moment but her voice was dull, as if it made little difference to her one way or the other.

"No, but he's going to need a good dentist. You'd better get up and come with me."

Elsie shook her head. "It isn't fair."

"What isn't fair? That four people have died who had nothing to do with your problems? That my father probably broke his leg a minute ago?" The hand that held the pistol shook with anger.

"I didn't want to come to American." Elsie ignored Percy's questions. "But we had no reason to stay in England. Evelyn felt if we came here, we could track him down, punish him for what he did to our parents."

"So you got jobs in his production, as an assistant stage manager and assistant wardrobe supervisor. I'm sure you know quite a bit about the running of a production, coming from a theatrical family such as yours."

"Not really." Elsie's voice was dreamlike, ethereal almost. "But one can learn. My father kept us as far away from the theatre as often as he could. He didn't think it was good enough for us. Ironic, isn't it? It wasn't until he died that some of his associates took pity on us and offered us jobs in small theatres around England. They knew we lost everything. We couldn't afford to stay in school any longer, between Dexter Wainwright stealing my mother's ideas for the musical and my father having jeopardized everything with his position in the war. He was a Nazi sympathizer, you know, but that didn't mean Wainwright should have poisoned him."

"You're sure he did?"

"I'm not sure of anything, anymore. Evelyn said he poisoned father, so he must have done." She put her head down again on her knees. "I'm so tired."

"I'll bet." She watched as Elsie lay down and curled up on the floor, her foot hitting a pill bottle. The bottle rolled a few feet toward Percy. The detective bend down, picked it up, and read the label.

"Seconal. That's a barbiturate." She shook the bottle. "Empty. How much of this did you take?" She went over to the girl and spoke in a louder voice. "Hey, Elsie, how much of this bottle did you take?"

"Enough," was the soft reply. "Enough."

Chapter Thirty-five

"Hey, Pop, how are you doing?" Percy poked her head inside the closed curtains of Pop's bed in the ward. Six beds to a room, and you were lucky at that. The main ward held thirty-two.

Percy expected to find Pop alone. Instead, a woman with curly platinum blonde hair and a slim figure bent over him, giving him a kiss on the face.

"Gee, I hope I'm not interrupting something. Actually, I hope I am." Percy threw back the curtain and stepping inside. The woman stood up, turned around, and looked at Percy with a grin on her face.

"S...Sera?" Percy stuttered. The woman was her kid sister, her usual long red hair now a shorter, white hot blonde. Despite being siblings, Percy and Sera looked as different as two women could, putting aside the fifteen-year difference in their ages. One topped five-foot eleven inches in height, the other five-foot two. Sera's frame was slender, while Percy was a well-cushioned gal. What they had in common until that day, was the paternal carrot red hair inherited, according to their deceased Uncle Gil, from their much heralded Norse ancestor, Eric the Red.

"Hi-de-ho, Percy!" Sera said. She patted at the blonde curly locks of her do with a proud hand. "Don't you just dig it? Am I a hep kitten, or what?"

Percy found herself speechless but managed a smile. After all, she adored her kid sister, if not all of the harebrained schemes Sera came up with from time to time.

"Serendipity has dyed her hair," Pop said unnecessarily. "Something about Betty Grable.

Sera strutted up and down the confines of the small curtained area, displaying not only the latest in hairdos but a newly purchased frock, tag still dangling from under one arm. Flared at the hemline when she twirled, the dress ended just below the knees, and hugged
her hips, waist and bust, 'not too much, but just enough' as Vogue would say. Small white flowers pattered on a teal background, emphasizing turquoise colored eyes that flashed with vitality.

Percy sported a tailored, wide-lapel, forest green pants suit, softened by a cream colored blouse. It was her Sunday best, but nothing was too good for the day she wrapped up her first case. She had actually brushed and styled her hair. Worn loose, soft curls trailed down the sides of her neck and back. She felt good about how she looked; a rare occurrence. Her own eyes, more pure green than her sister's, radiated their own vitality and more. A sharp confidence.

"And it only cost six dollars and fifty-seven cents, including tip," Sera bragged about her new hairstyle.

"You paid for that?" Percy caught herself. "I mean, what did you pay for that dress? You might want to cut off the tag, Sera, before you wear it out of here."

Sera stopped twirling and in a panic, began to search the dress on her body. "Oh, no! Daniel's waiting outside to take me to the movies! Where's the tag, Percy? Help me."

Percy stepped forward, lifted Sera's right arm, grabbed the tag and gave a yank. It came off in her hand along with the string.

Sera snatched at it. "Thanks. I got it on sale at Macy's, half price!"

"I keep telling her that her hair looks like cotton candy I once had at the County Fair." Pop grabbed one of the handles above his bed to pull himself up into a more comfortable position. "But nobody's listening to me."

He wore his favorite striped pajamas from home, Mother having cut open and sacrificed one leg to accommodate the thigh to ankle cast. Encased in the thick plaster, his right leg stuck straight out and hung from above on a pulley system not unlike the one at the Royal. Five swollen pink toes moved independently as he struggled to get comfortable.

"Here, Pop." Percy went to the other side of the bed. She puffed up his pillows and stacked them to support his back. "Better?"

"Yes," he growled, obviously still upset over his youngest daughter's choice in hair color. "I don't see what's wrong with leaving Mother Nature alone, Serendipity. You don't see your sister changing her hair --"

"Oooooh, Pop," Percy drawled in a low voice. "Leave me out of this."

"Now see here, Pop." Sera announcement was made grandly. "I'm a grownup woman and I make my own money. I can do what I --"

"In that case, you can start paying rent." Her father crossed his arms over his chest and glared at her. "Just like your sister does."

A shocked look crossed Sera's face. Her jaw dropped open and she gasped noisily.

"Don't want to get pulled into this." Percy muttered to no one in particular.

"I don't make that much money down at the munitions factory," Sera protested. "And you know I'm saving it to go to beauty school." She turned to her older sister. "Tell him, Percy. You know I'm right. Tell him."

"Isn't anybody going to leave me out of this?" Percy directed her comment to a lone plant sitting on the windowsill.

"Nobody has to tell me anything, young lady." Pop's voice rose above his two daughters. "I am your father and the head of the household. If I say --"

"Hey," a caustic voice yelled over the curtains. "You want to keep it down to a dull roar in there? Some of us are trying to sleep!"

"Sorry." All three Cole's spoke in unison then looked at one another, and broke out in embarrassed laughter. Sera came to the head of the bed and looked down at her father, her demeanor changing from belligerence to submissiveness.

"Gee, Pop, I'm not trying to make a grandstand play about this but, come on, paying rent." Sera whined at the end.

"I think two dollars a week is fair, Serendipity, for room and board. That's including three square meals a day." Pop's tone was firm.

"You mean, you're charging me more for Mother's cooking? I never thought of them as square. How about if I don't eat at home and we..." Sera broke off when she saw the looks on both their faces. "I guess not." Sera let out a groan.

"It's like you say, Serendipity." Pop straightened his covers in an authoritative way. "If you're old enough to start dying your hair, you're old enough to contribute to the household. Now you run along to wherever it is you're going. But don't you be coming home too late. Mother has enough to contend with."

"I'm going to the movies with Daniel. Casablanca. It's so romantic." She let out a deep sigh. "I've already seen it four times.
Just once, I'd like Humphrey Bogart to get on the plane with Ingrid Bergman at the end. Later, gator." She grabbed her black wool jacket, pushed aside the curtain, and flounced out. Percy and Pop watched her departing figure.

Pop looked at Percy. "She gets that from your mother's side of the family."

"I don't know, Pop. We both got our red hair from Uncle Gil. I even got his height. So it could be your side." Percy looked at her father and blew him a quick kiss. "How's your leg, Pop? Honest now."

He reached for the stirrup-like straps again, pulled up, and adjusted himself. "I'm a mite uncomfortable, Persephone, I admit it."

"Well, no wonder. A leg broke in three places? I'd be uncomfortable, too. Have you been taking your pain killers?"

"Not unless I have to, child. They tend to make me groggy." He made an obvious change of subjects. "You just missed your brother. Adjudication was telling me he's taken on another case. His practice is starting to pick up."

"Good. Where's Mother?"

"She's home making me an apple, carrot, and parsnip pie."

"I'm sorry, Pop."

"Something new she's fiddling with. Your mother means well." He shrugged and picked up his spirits. "You've been gone all day. Where were you?"

"The police station with Mick and then the theatre. They're going on with the show, Pop, just as if nothing happened."

"No."

"Yes."

"Nothing stops show folks, does it?" Pop shook his head in disbelief.

"Naw. They're as bad as detectives."

Father and daughter guffawed for a moment.

"You sit right down here and tell me what's been going on." Pop patted the side of his bed. She perched on the edge. "I'm proud of you, Persephone, although I still don't know how you did it."

"Considering all the secrets everybody was keeping and that damned headache, I didn't think I'd ever figure it out."

"But you did and that's all that matters."

"I guess, Pop, but not before more people got hurt. Although I now understand how outside forces can influence your thinking. I need to watch that in the future. I should have figured this one out in a couple of hours."

"But how did you do it, child? How did you do it?" He repeated the question with eagerness.

"I kept coming back to motive and opportunity. And then something kept nagging at me from the beginning, but I couldn't bring it forward."

"What was that?"

"John Wayne."

"The actor?"

"Yeah. His real first name is Marion. Sera mentioned it the other night and it stuck in the back of my mind, but I didn't know why. Then I realized yesterday, nowhere did any paperwork actually say Jacob Cohen's two children were females. I *assumed* they were, given the two first names, Elsie and Evelyn. But Evelyn is a fairly common name for either sex in England. It meant I could have been looking for two women or *a man* and a woman."

"Elsie a name not being used for baby boys."

"Not that I know of. Talk about red herrings. At first I thought Mavis was really Elsie. I spent a lot of time looking at Wainwright's private secretary."

"Actually," Pop said, going on with his theme, "I'm not too fond of it being used for a girl, either. I mean, Elsie." He said the name with a look of distaste on his face.

"This from the man who named his two daughters Persephone and Serendipity. Not to mention calling his son Adjudication."

"My children happen to have beautiful, albeit unusual, names." Pop's tone was defensive. "Mother and I stand by --"

"All right, all right, Pop. We're off the track. Apologies for derailing us."

"Many a soul," he went on as if not interrupted, "has said to me how much they appreciate the time and effort Mother and I put into choosing your names."

"Those are the ones who named their own children Tom, Dick, and Harry, no doubt." She looked at her father and laughed. "I'm just razzing you, Pop. Should I go on with my story?"

He gave his head a quick nod but looked away. "Just don't be picking on my choice in children's names, young lady."

Percy studied her father for a moment. His face was a little flushed and eyes dilated. "Pop, we should check your medications. You don't look quite right."

"Ahhh, it's my leg. It's paining me something awful. I'm sorry, child." He patted Percy on the hand. "I been fighting it, but you'd better give me those pills I hid in the drawer there." He pointed to the side table.

Percy opened the drawer, took out a small white, container with pills, and passed them to him. "You hid the pills you were supposed to take from the nurse, huh?" She poured water into a glass and handed it to her father.

"Something like that. You go on with what you were saying, Persephone. I'm all ears." He swallowed the pills. "All this time you was looking for two females, not realizing Elsie was a woman and Evelyn a man."

"Right. Spelled the same but for a man, Evelyn is pronounced with a long 'e', like the 'e' in evening. Once I thought about 'what's in a name', I saw that the stage manager had access to every place in the theatre without raising any eyebrows. And the assistant wardrobe supervisor had access to all sorts of costumes, like a nurse's uniform. On another note, did you know Mick found the truck Evelyn rented a couple of weeks ago?"

Pop shook his head, paying rapt attention to Percy's words.

"Evelyn wore one of the false beards out of the hair department when he tried to run down Felicity Dowell. When that didn't work, one of them poisoned her tea. When *that* didn't work, Elsie sent her a threatening letter. According to Evelyn's confession, they'd used one or two of those tactics the week before on the three actors who did leave. They had to pull out the stops to get an actress playing a role as good as Lady Macbeth to leave the show, though."

"They tried to hide everything they were doing under the witch's curse and the pranks Sir Anthony was pulling." Pop shook his head.

"And they initially succeeded. Evelyn admitted he'd cut the rope for the sandbag, hoping it would land on Sir Anthony, but when it got the stage manager instead, it was even better. He now completely controlled the backstage area. These Cohen kids were determined to do anything and everything to close the show."

"How was he able to say that? I thought you near broke his jaw."

"But I didn't, though, just loosened a few of his teeth. Some things he wrote out, some things he muttered through the bandages. Now that it's over, he's become cooperative. Especially…" Percy broke off and looked down.

"They didn't seem very English to me, either one, when I was talking to them." Pop didn't notice the expression on his daughter's face.

"That was the devil of it, Pop." Percy forced a smile and turned back to her father. "I mean, you and I, we sound like where we come from. But people in the theatre do all sorts of accents. The second Lady Macbeth is American and her English accent is very posh. So which side of the pond they *sounded* like they came from didn't matter a hill of beans."

"What about the partial print on the binoculars? Anything come of that?"

"Too blurred, but fortunately, Evelyn has confessed to everything."

Pop reached over and lightly caressed Percy's hand. "What's happening with the girl, Elsie? Were they able to save her?"

Percy shook her head. Her voice was emotionless. "She didn't make it, Pop. By the time they could get up to the catwalk, bring her down, and pump her stomach, she was too far gone. She died early this morning. I told them as soon as I got down from the catwalk, Pop. But she took so many pills." Percy looked away.

"It's not your fault. I don't think with the way everything turned out, she wanted to live. I am sorry. She may have pushed me off that catwalk but for such a young girl to die, needlessly...." He stopped talking and gave out a tsk tsk in disapproval, shaking his head, too.

"I know. It is sad. But she wasn't all that innocent, Pop, no matter how much she looked like Alice in Wonderland. Elsie's the one who disguised herself as a nurse and put the poison in Laverne's IV. And she probably poisoned Felicity Dowell's tea, too. For certain, she wrote the letters and helped start the fire in the uptown rooming house. Two elderly people died in that, more innocent than Elsie will ever be."

"How did they manage to plan all this from day to day? They weren't ever together, were they?"

"No, they thought it was too risky. They were never in each other's company, except when they could put their heads together, as Ned said, pretending to be boyfriend and girlfriend. But they couldn't do that too often, so they communicated via notes. I found a stack hidden in a locked drawer in the stage manager's prompt station. They're pretty interesting reading, although I don't come out so good in them. They found me bovine and fat. Which is okay, Pop. They underestimated me. It gave me an element of surprise with them."

"What are you talking about? They tried to kill you with the archway."

"Yeah, but before that they left me pretty much alone. You should see the passports Mick took from both their places. I don't know where they bought them, but they looked genuine enough. Those two kids must have been planning this a long time. Every dime they had left from their parent's estate went into trying to pay Wainwright back for what he did to them. And look at them now, one dead and the other going to jail for the rest of his life." She let out a troubled sigh. "Some days it doesn't pay to get up in the morning."

"You see some justice in what they tried to do?"

"No, Pop. Here's a part you don't know. Mick spoke with Scotland Yard today and it seems that Mrs. Cohen was suspected of poisoning her husband. There was a diary they found right after she killed herself and because she was already dead, they didn't pursue it. In it she said she couldn't live with what she did, even though Cohen deserved to die for betraying his heritage. Neither Mick nor I wanted to tell Evelyn, but someday he'll have to know. This whole thing isn't as clean as I'd like it to be."

"I know what you mean, child."

They both sat in silence for a moment then Pop plucked at his blanket before speaking. "Persephone, I'm not one to tell you what to do --"

"Since when?"

"But I am your father." Pop went on as if she hadn't interrupted. "I want you to stop this detecting nonsense and either go back to being a secretary or ---"

It was Percy's turn to interrupt him. "What are you talking about? I solved the case, didn't I? I'm good at this, Pop."

"Being good has nothing to do with it." His voice grew stronger with his beliefs. "This is dangerous work. Look what happened." He gestured to his broken leg.

"Yes, but not to me, Pop. It happened to you."

"But it could have just as easily been you," he said defiantly. "Now don't argue with me. I knew no good could come of Gilleathain taking you all those years to target practice using that German Mauser. Leaving it to you in his will and all. I knew we were asking for trouble."

"Uncle Gil taught me to be a crackerjack shot, Pop. It helped give me a lot of self-confidence."

"A little too much, as far as I can see. No matter. I don't want you doing this anymore. You did well, Persephone; I'm not denying it. I'm proud of you. But it's over, done with. And no daughter of mine is going to be doing such dangerous work. I could never live with myself." He looked away, the last words reverberating within the small curtained area.

"I tell you what, Pop." Percy took a softer, easier tone. "Let's table this discussion for now. You're laid up and someone's got to run the business. For instance, I need to break down the costs and type up the bill for Dexter Wainwright."

"What's the final reckoning?"

"One day's work at fifteen bucks and two day's at twenty-five –"

"You're charging him for today, Percy?" Pop interjected. "That don't seem right."

"I'm still on the case, Pop, and so are you. Aren't we discussing it this very minute? He needs to be charged for that. How are we going to get Cole Investigations back in the black if we don't? And we saved the S.O.B.'s life, Pop. Given who he is, it doesn't count for much but it counts for something."

"I see your point, Persephone." He patted her hand and smiled at her.

"All right then. So I'm charging him sixty-five bucks plus expenses."

"What expenses?" Pop turned sharply to her with a quizzical look on his face.

"Three pastrami sandwiches, for one thing. Don't worry, Pop. I'm always fair, even if I shave it a little in our favor now and again."

"That's my girl." He chortled.

"Okay. So after I wind up this case, I thought I'd look into the synagogue vandals for you."

"Oh, no," Pop protested, shaking his head.

"You left some good notes, Pop. It's a shame to leave the rabbis hanging like this, especially with you being laid up and all. Because," she added, "after reading what you wrote, I think you're right."

"Oh, no you don't. You're not winning me over with your sweet talk." Pop shook his head again vehemently then stopped to ask, "You think I'm right?"

"I do. It's one of those two Nazi sympathizers, for sure. Only I don't think it's the older one. I think it's the squirt."

"Exactly my thoughts. Great minds think alike, Persephone." He pointed a finger at his daughter with pride. "He's always around, looking innocent, but listening in to what we're doing and saying. I've had my eye on him."

"So after I turn in the bill to Wainwright, get the refrigerator fixed, and take Oliver trick or treating, Cole Investigations is back on the case." She stood and straightened up Pop's bed clothes.

"You'll keep me informed every step of the way, Persephone. And it's just until I get back on my feet."

"You bet. Then we'll have a nice, long talk." Percy kissed her father on the forehead. "You rest now, Pop. I'll visit tomorrow." She picked up the end of the divider curtain, set to flip it around her as she left, but paused for a moment. "Oh, Pop, keep your eyes out that window. I'm bringing Oliver by so you can see him in his pirate's costume before we set out trick or treating. We'll stand under that streetlight across the street. Around five p.m. We'll wave up to you."

"Something to look forward to, Persephone."

"Love you, Pop."

"Love you more."

Chapter Thirty-six

Percy pulled Ophelia into the empty spot in front of the apartment building. This tenement on Houston Street, like many others throughout the lower east side, was a place where family knew family, sometimes for generations. Since Pop bought the black Dodge back in nineteen twenty-nine, this spot was where he liked to park the car. Unless someone was visiting from another neighborhood and didn't know better, this parking space was always left for the Coles. Percy turned off the motor, rolled up the windows, picked up the heavy bag at her side, and got out of the car.

Barely four o'clock but All Hallows Eve, children were already dressed in costumes, roaming up and down the street, clutching various sized bags of easily-won candy. Percy waved to a mother herding eight small children, all dressed in handmade, but clever costumes. Some costumes looked like they took fifteen minutes, such as Casper the Friendly Ghost, and others, like a gypsy dressed in a brocade vest and skirt covered with golden spangles, took hours. Knowing the mother, they were all labors of love.

Percy smiled as a three-year old toddled down the street dressed as a large pumpkin, holding the hand of her older brother, a fairly nifty version of the Green Lantern. Percy was glad Oliver had decided not to go as that character. She'd counted three of them since she got out of the car.

She'd been so engrossed in watching the swarms of costumed children, Percy hadn't noticed the nattily dressed man sitting on her stoop holding a large bouquet of multi-colored flowers. As she approached the steps, Dexter Wainwright rose and proffered the flowers to her.

She didn't take them, but tried to smile. "Mr. Wainwright, how did you know I was here?"

"I called the hospital and spoke to Pop. He said you were on your way home, so I thought I'd come and wait for you."

"I see. It's just that I'm surprised you came down here. I thought you were rehearsing for tonight's opening."

"They don't need me there now that you took care of the bad guys." He gave her a wink.

If one more person winks at me, I might have to start swinging.

Not being able to read her mind, the producer went on. "Hugo is whipping the cast into shape as we speak. Everything is going swimmingly, except my secretary gave her two-week notice today." He cocked his head, his eyes piercing into hers. "You know anything about that?"

"Nope."

"Would you tell me if you did?"

Percy shook her head mutely.

"Too bad. She said I should give you a bonus for saving the show. I told her I hired you to do that, but wondered where her idea came from."

"People get ideas." Percy's tone was noncommittal.

"Did I tell you Felicity is back in the show?"

"No kidding."

"She got a telegram from Olivier last night. Seems the theatre he was hoping to use for Medea got damaged in an air raid day before yesterday. Larry's production is off and mine is back on."

"What about this Cynthia? The one who stepped into the role? What happens to her?"

Wainwright shrugged, as if he hadn't given it a thought until that moment. "She goes back as understudy, I guess, and whatever else she was doing in the show."

"You're in, you're out, huh?"

"Oh, they're used to it. Actors, you know, get used to anything."

Percy shook her head. "Man, they need a union."

"They have one, my dear. Actors' Equity. According to them, we have to pay her some kind of compensation, that's all." Wainwright looked at her and winked again.

"You ought to check that tic in your right eye." Percy looked at her watch. "If you'll excuse me, I was about to go in and get the invoice ready. I'll mail it to you tomorrow." She shuffled the large paper bag she was carrying into the other arm. "Was there something else you wanted?"

Wordless but with a grand smile, he thrust the flowers at her again.

"Are these for Pop? I'll be sure to give them to him."

"They're for you, actually." He looked her up and down. "You look nice."

"Me?" Puzzled, she shrugged and took the flowers. "Thanks, Mr. Wainwright. I'll send you your bill and, well..." She fought for something to say. "Have a nice life." Brushing by him on the stairs, she took a step up to the stoop.

He laid a hand on her arm as she swept by and tightened his grip. "Percy I hope you don't mind if I call you that after all we've been through together."

"Depends." She narrowed her eyes on his face, pausing with one leg on the next step.

He smiled at her, teeth flashing in the sunlight. He gave her arm a gentle tug and clutching the flowers in one arm and the bag in the other, she stepped down to the same tread as his.

One of the tenants in the building clamored up the steps with two small children wearing carefully-made costumes. The smaller girl was dressed as a witch, and the larger girl as Dorothy from the Wizard of Oz. Percy pulled away from Wainwright to let them in between. Awkwardly, the producer also stepped aside, allowing the family to pass up the center of the steps and into the building.

Percy took the opportunity to leave, as well. She bounded up the steps, pivoting around on the stoop. "I'll see that Pop gets these flowers, Wainwright," she said, with an air of finality.

"Percy!" He called up to her, his voice plaintive on the one word.

"What is it?" Her eyebrows furrowed again in puzzlement.

"I…I need your help." Dejected, he sat down on one of the lower steps, wringing his hands that lay in his lap.

"I'm probably going to regret this," she said, as she came down the steps and sat beside him, "but okay, shoot." Percy set the bag and flowers by her side.

"It's my wife."

"Excuse me?"

"I think she's seeing someone." His body jerked around a little, as if the subject was too uncomfortable for him to talk about and sit still.

"And," Percy prompted.

"And I want you to look into it."

"You mean like what? Follow her around? See if it's true?" He nodded looking down at his feet.

Percy blew out air, thinking. "I guess I could do that. I'm tied up in Brooklyn for the next day or so, but after that I could tail her, see what's what."

Wainwright cheered up visibly. He threw his arm around Percy's shoulder and drew her to him. She looked over at the arm pulling at her. She pulled away. He didn't seem to notice.

"I knew you'd help me out, Percy. She and I, well, we've drifted apart recently. Gone our separate ways. She never did understand me, even when we were getting along."

It was as if every red flag inside Percy's head began to wave. "Uh-huh. Your wife doesn't understand you."

"No." He shook his head vigorously. "She never really did. Ours was not a good marriage. I'm lonely." His brown eyes stared into her green eyes ones, searching for something. "You know how that is."

"I do." Percy broke free and shot up to a standing position. "I think I'll renege on that offer to tail your wife. Doesn't sound like something Cole Investigations wants to do."

Wainwright also stood and grabbed hold of her near the elbow. Percy looked down at her arm and then up into the producer's smiling face.

"You want to let go?" Her voice was low, her tone careful. He lightened his touch on her arm.

"I've been very impressed with how you handled this case, Percy." Wainwright smiled at her again. "I've been impressed with you."

"Good. You can recommend us to your friends. We could use the business. If that's all…" She turned to leave. Wainwright grabbed her arm again, this time not so gently.

"You've got five seconds to stop doing that." She faced him. "I don't like it when people touch me uninvited."

Smiling in what he seemed to think was a winning way, he threw both arms around her.

"Are you kidding me with this out here in the middle of the street?" Her eyes darted around her and back at him is disbelief.

"Percy, sweetheart," he cajoled, leaving his arms where they were. "You feel what's going on between us, I know you do. It's been there from the beginning. Let's go somewhere

where we can be alone." Wainwright waggled an eyebrow. "There's something about a tough gal that is surprisingly attractive." He puckered up, attempting to give her a kiss.

"You know, you're right." Percy gave him a big smile. "I *am* a tough gal." She pulled away from him, swung her arm back, and hit him with her closed fist as hard as she could.

Stunned, Wainwright stumbled backward, bounced off the railing then fell to the steps, blood spurting from of his nose.

One on the old schnozzola, as Jimmy Durante would say. Aim perfect, follow-through impeccable. Uncle Gil would have been proud.

"That felt good and was long overdue." She opened and closed her hand. "I'm going to have swollen knuckles for a few days, but it was worth it."

Caught up in the drama, a sparse applause broke out from some of her neighbors, who had been either watching the proceedings or strolling by. The producer looked from them to Percy in shock.

"Why you bitch," Wainwright cried out, reaching inside a breast pocket for his handkerchief. "You can't go around hitting people." He pulled himself into a sitting position and held the hanky under his bleeding nose.

"Sure I can. I just did."

"See if you get any money out of me now, Persephone Cole. You just see." He screamed up at her, a nasty look on his face.

"Listen, you," she growled, stepping in between his sprawled out legs, and hauling him up by his shirt collar into a standing position. Nearby neighbors cheered randomly, as they looked on. This was better than the Macy's Thanksgiving Day Parade.

"Don't get me any madder than I already am. You made a forward pass, and you got intercepted by a right hook.

Take it like a man." She put her face closer to his. "And you *are* going to pay Cole Investigations exactly what you owe us or my good friend, Walter Winchell, is going to hear all about you running your scared ass down that catwalk while I, a lily-white lady, saved your bacon." She took a deep breath and let the thought sink in. "Might be good publicity for Cole Investigations."

It was another one of her distortions of the truth. For one thing, it was unethical to betray client confidentiality, and she would never do that. But Wainwright, not having any ethics, might not know where ethics started or where they left off. Secondly, she met Walter Winchell only once, along with three hundred other people, when he was signing autographs in Herald Square.

Okay, I only saw him once, but that information would be splitting hairs with a guy like Dexter Wainwright.

Wainwright's face told her the gamble paid off. He seemed to be nonplussed by the statement. His face blanched of any color left to it after getting his nose busted. The producer pulled free without saying anything, moved past her, and down the steps onto the sidewalk.

"I'll expect the check in the mail, no delays." Percy watched him as he hurried down the sidewalk.

Wainwright didn't say anything but waved his hand holding the bloody handkerchief and nodded at the same time, acknowledging he'd heard her, but without a backward glance.

She bent down, picking up the paper bag and bouquet from the steps. "Thanks for the flowers," she called after him.

Percy shook her head as she took the final steps up the stoop. The ground floor window opened wide and Mrs. Goldberg leaned her head out, wiping flour-covered hands on a red and white checked apron.

"Persela, darling," she said in her heavy Yiddish accent, pronouncing the word 'darling' like 'dah-link'. "You are going to get into trouble one of these days if you keep going around with the slugging. Your brother, the lawyer, says it isn't legal."

"Ordinarily, I would agree with him, Mrs. Goldberg. But every now and then, you gotta do what you gotta do."

"And mazel tov. How is your father, darling?"

"The doctors say he's going to be fine." Percy sniffed the air. "What's that I smell baking? Your famous apple pie?"

"There's a slice waiting for you and your sweet Oliver, when it cools off. Only don't tell your mother. The world is already at war."

Percy laughed. "Thanks. Can't wait. Maybe we'll stop by after I take Oliver trick or treating. Have a nice evening." Percy opened the front door of the apartment building and stepped into the hallway.

"If you say so, darling, if you say so." She heard Mrs. Goldberg call after her then shut the window.

Chapter Thirty-seven

"Hello in there!" Percy yelled as she opened the apartment door. "Anybody home?"

The kitchen door swung open and the small boy who meant everything to Percy bounded forward. Percy set the package and flowers on the small, inept hall table that ever threatened to collapse, and bent down to grab the running boy, opening her arms wide.

"Mommy, Mommy!" Oliver ran into her waiting arms. "You're home!" He gave her a quick embrace then struggled free. "Look what grandmother made for me." He spun around in his pirate's costume. Black pants, torn in long strips at the hems, a white blousy shirt with puffy sleeves, and red cummerbund dressed him. His dark hair was covered by a red bandana. The look was completed by a plastic sword shoved in at the waistband.

"Well, shiver me timbers. If it isn't Long John Silvers." Percy used her best Wallace Beery voice from Treasure Island.

"You should see my eye patch," Oliver exclaimed. "I can't see out of it though."

Mother pushed the kitchen door open and ambled down the hall to her daughter and grandson still by the front door. Her hair was free again, white and wild, and except for the intelligent sparkle in her brown eyes and the smile on her face, she did look like a walking Dandelion. Percy stood to greet her mother.

"Mother, thank you so much."

"Oh, stop it, Persephone." Mother waved away her daughter's gratitude. "If a grandmother can't do something like this for her grandson, what good is it all?"

Percy knelt down in front of her son, guilt overtaking her. "I'm sorry about the parrot, Oliver. With all I've been doing I just didn't have time --"

"Grandma made me a parrot," Oliver interrupted.

"She did?" Percy looked at her mother.

"It was supposed to be a surprise for you." Mother grinned. "I sewed it out of scraps and stuffed it with polyfoam."

"It looks really real." Oliver thought about it for a moment then added, "From a distance."

"I'll bet it does." Percy pushed some of his bangs under the bandana. "Maybe I didn't do anything for your Halloween costume but…" She stopped speaking and went to the large paper bag on the table. "I did manage to get our jack-'o-lantern back." She pulled the medium size carved pumpkin out of the bag and showed it to her mother and son.

"Wow! Where did you find it, Mommy?" Oliver looked at his mother with open admiration.

"Oh, it just wandered away for a moment. You know how Halloween can be full of witches' trickery. Why don't you put it back outside before we leave to go trick or treating?" She turned to Mother. "Did Father Patrick call?"

"Yes. He said the three boys were there and all was well."

"But Mommy," Oliver protested, the expression on his face troubled.

"What is it, Oliver?" Percy turned back to her son and set the pumpkin back on the table.

"I'm too big to go trick or treating with my mother. I was supposed to go with Freddy, remember? But him and his mom took the train to see his father today."

"*He* and his mom, Oliver," Percy corrected, automatically.

"They went to Fort Bragg, North Carolina. Or is it South Carolina?" Mother looked confused.

"North."

"But it's still in the south, right?" Mother smiled at her daughter and grandson.

"Yes, ma'am." Both Percy and Oliver answered simultaneously.

Mother looked relieved. "Sylvia says they're going to stay there until her husband's release from the hospital, in about a week."

"Good." She looked down at her son. "Well, maybe you're too big to go trick or treating with your mother, young man." Percy went into the bag again. "But how about going with a witch?" She pulled out the nose, chin, gown, and hat she wore in Macbeth. She shook them out then held them up for her son to see.

Oliver's eyes got large and he took in a sharp breath. "Ooooo!" Excitement colored his voice. "It *does* look like a witch's
costume, Mommy. Are you going as the bad witch from the Wizard of Oz?"

"Is that your favorite bad witch?"

"Yeah!" Oliver jumped up and down.

"Then that's the one." Percy turned to her mother. "My friend, Elizabeth, pilfered this for me from the show. Actually, they were throwing it out. The dress is ripped and the hat got crushed when I jumped off the platform, but I think it only adds more character, don't you?"

Mother took the torn gown from Percy's hands.

"What happened to the knuckles on your right hand, Persephone?" Mother's tone was quiet.

"Ran into a brick wall. I'll soak my hand in some ice, if we have any."

"The refrigerator repairman came a short while ago and fixed it. It should be cool in an hour or so. The bill's on the counter. Meanwhile, Sera brought some ice home, if you want it. It's in the ice chest. Does the brick wall have a name?"

"Mother, sometimes you're too sharp for me."

Mother grunted and gave the gown the practiced onceover of a seamstress. "A tuck here, a stitch there, and I think this will hold together enough for you to wear tonight. The hat is beyond redemption, but we can tie it on your head. How are you supposed to keep that nose and chin on your face, Persephone?"

"Ta da!" Percy pulled out a small bottle of glue from the bag. "And here's some green greasepaint to cover my face."

"Neato," cried Oliver. "You're going to be really ugly. The best witch ever."

"That I am, Oliver. But first, let's take this pumpkin and set it back in the hall again. This way all the kids will know to stop by our door to trick or treat tonight."

"Can I do it?" Oliver reached out. Percy placed the pumpkin in his outstretched arms and with a serious stride, Oliver went out into the hallway. Mother and grandmother watched him.

"I told Pop we'd stop by and stand outside the hospital before we went trick or treating so he could see Oliver's costume," Percy said in barely more than a whisper. "It will give him a good laugh to see me standing there, the world's tallest witch."

"That's very thoughtful, dear. You're a good daughter."

"You going to be all right, handing out the candy without Pop this year?" Percy turned an anxious face to her mother.

"I wouldn't miss it. And afterward, I'll go to the hospital and spend the night with your father, like I did last night. The nurses are very nice. They even brought in a cot for me to sleep on."

"Then Happy Halloween, Mother. As Shakespeare said, 'All's Well That Ends Well'. It's not Macbeth, but it'll do."

≈

About Heather Haven

After studying drama at the University of Miami in Miami, Florida, Heather went to Manhattan to pursue a career. There she wrote short stories, novels, comedy acts, television treatments, ad copy, commercials, and two one-act plays, produced at several places, such as Playwrights Horizon. Once she even ghostwrote a book on how to run an employment agency. She was unemployed at the time.

Her first novel of the Alvarez Family Murder Mysteries, ***Murder is a Family Business***, is winner of the Single Titles Reviewers' Choice Award 2011, and the second, ***A Wedding to Die For,*** received the 2012 finalist nods from both Global and EPIC's Best eBook Mystery of the Year. The third of the series, ***Death Runs in the Family***, recently debuted and has also been nominated for EPIC's Best eBook Mystery of the Year.

Heather's most recent endeavor is the 1940s holiday mystery series starring a five-foot eleven, full-figured gal named Persephone Cole. 'Percy' Cole has the same hard-boiled, take-no-prisoners attitude as Sam Spade, Lew Archer, and Phillip Marlow, but tops it off with a wicked sense of humor. The Persephone Cole Vintage Mystery Series takes place during World War II, three thousand miles and sixty-odd years away from the California Alvarez Family Murder Mystery series.

Also by Heather Haven

•***Death of a Clown*** **–** A noir mystery

The Alvarez Family Murder Mystery Series

•*Murder is a Family Business* – Book One

•*A Wedding to Die For* – Book Two

•*Death Runs in the Family* – Book Three

The Persephone Cole Vintage Mystery Series

•*Iced Diamonds* – Book Two

Read on for a sample of *Iced Diamonds*!

Iced Diamonds
Chapter One

"Are you that fat lady detective?" The male voice spoke in a hurried manner on the other end of the line.

I don't know about being a lady, Percy thought, *being born and raised on the lower east side, but I am substantial and a PI. So two out of three ain't bad.*

"Yeah, that's me, Persephone Cole. Although, I would have preferred to be called full-figured, plump, stout, portly, hefty, zaftig, rotund, corpulent, chubby, or how about roly-poly? Something with a little thought in it. But who's this and what do you want?" She pulled a small bag of pistachio nuts out of the pocket of her slacks with her free hand, tossed the bag on the telephone table, and routed around for a nut, while she listened.

"My name's Waller, William Waller--"

"Like Fats Waller?" she interrupted, grabbing a salty nut out of the bag. *Okay, you unimaginative creep. We can all make fat cracks.* The other end of the line went stone, cold silent.

Percy popped the nut in her mouth and using years of practice, separated the two shells with her front teeth, and sucked out the meat. She picked the two shells out of her mouth and chewed, as she dropped the shells into one of the ubiquitous ashtrays scattered around the apartment for this sole purpose.

A sudden loud voice coming from the kitchen radio crackled an announcement of the need to buy war bonds. The United States had been in the war for over a year now and most everyone was tapped out, but the voice droned on, just in case.

"Hold it a minute, Waller," Percy commanded. She cradled the phone against what has been referred to from time to time as her ample bosom, and shouted down the hall of the railroad flat to the kitchen.

"Hey, shut that door, will you, Pop? I got a potential client here." The swinging door swooshed closed between the hallway and the kitchen. Uncle Sam had been muted, at least for the moment.

Percy put the phone back to her ear to the sound of heavy breathing. If she hadn't known better, she would have thought it was an obscene phone call.

"I'm back. What can I do for you, Mr. Waller?" She tried to keep her voice pleasant and professional, but it may have been a little too late for that. She reached for another nut.

"There's a dead elf in my storefront window."

"Excuse me?" Her hand froze midway to her mouth.

"One of those Santa elves from down the street. You know, Santa Land. I want to know what he's doing in my display window."

"Off the top of my head, I'd say not much, him being dead and all." This remark also met stony silence. "Never mind. Have you called the police?" She threw the nut back into the bag.

"Yes, they're here now. I never saw him before." His tone at first sounded puzzled then it changed. 'You're a real smarty pants, aren't you?"

"That's what they tell me." *Never give a jerk an even break, that's my motto.* "So why are you calling me if the cops are taking care of it? How'd you get my number?"

He lowered his voice. "I want to hire you, but I need to talk to you about this in person, not over the phone."

"I don't come cheap, Mr. Waller." *Actually, I do come cheap, but I'm about to hike up the price for you, buster. Fat, huh?*

We'll see about that. "I'm twenty a day plus expenses, with a three-day guarantee."

Percy paused, having trouble believing what she was asking, herself, and added, "It being the holiday season and all, I'll make it a two-day guarantee. But it's still twenty bucks a day."

"Very well, Mrs. Cole, whatever you say. Just get here." The words came out rapidly, and in what Miss Schultz, her English teacher, might have called a 'terse manner'.

"It's *Miss* Cole and where's here?"

"Fifty-ninth and Fifth Avenue, right off Central Park. Waller and Sons Jewelry."

"I'll be there as soon as I can."

He paused, mumbled "Thank you," and disconnected.

She cradled the receiver on her shoulder. The last-minute attempt at manners on his part surprised her, even though the address he gave was in a pretty hoity-toity part of Manhattan.

I should have stuck to the three-day minimum.

She hung up the phone with gusto and the rickety telephone table her mother insisted on calling 'dainty' wobbled and nearly fell over. Since she could remember, this genuine knock-off of an exact replica of a Louis the Sixteenth, had been hanging out in the hallway of their lower eastside apartment threatening to collapse. Her mother inherited it from her favorite aunt and despite both women's tender ministrations and conviction of its value; Percy suspected its demise was eminent while its net worth was about thirty-nine cents.

She snatched up the bag of nuts, crammed them in her pocket, turned around in the narrow vestibule and took a quick gander at her reflection in the matching knock-off mirror. The bulge of the nuts only added to the bulges everywhere else. She loved Marlene Dietrich-style pant suits but they only came so big. When last weighed, Percy came in at 172 pounds. At five foot eleven inches, she often piled her hair on top of her head, gaining another three inches of height.

This made her taller than any woman she'd met and most of the men serving overseas in Hitler's war games. At thirty-five years of age, Percy preferred to think of herself as impressive, even in her Marlene Dietrich-style pant suit, which had been let down as well as being let out.

A quick scrutiny of her face made her wince. Without makeup, blondish-orange eyebrows and eyelashes looked almost nonexistent. In fact, her unhealthy pasty look was of someone living in a cave, year after year, never seeing the light of day. It was the usual redhead's plight.

One of the best inventions, in Percy's opinion, was cake mascara. She still had hers from high school, circa nineteen twenty-four, a testament to its longevity and her rare usage. Percy toyed with going into the bathroom, lathering it up, and applying some.

Naw, this is good enough for jazz.

She shook her head and long curls trapped in the rubber band at the crown of her head flopped everywhere. Red and amber-streaked ringlets shimmered in the light coming in from the lone window of the vestibule. Even she knew her thick red hair was one of her best features.

But only when it's under control, kiddo, and that's not today; too much moisture in the air. Maybe I can add Pop's fedora to my mop before I leave, so I don't have to think about it.

She headed to the kitchen which bustled with the usual early morning activity. The radio blared in the background, her father sat in his wheelchair with his bad leg resting straight out in its cast and him yelling at her younger sister.

"Serendipity, do you have to do that here?" Pop leaned in as far forward in the wheelchair as his belly and leg would permit. "And while we're eating breakfast? That smell is enough to drop flies. Now put that away. And pay attention to me when I'm talking to you."

Better known as Sera, Percy's kid sister ignored their father and continued to apply red lacquer to short, squat nails. Percy had the same short squat nails and wouldn't dream of bringing attention to them, but that was Sera.

Ignoring the uproar, Mother stood at the stove humming a tuneless but annoying little ditty. Percy's eight-year old son, Oliver, sat at the end of the table, hunched over his oatmeal, short, blue-black hair plastered down from the morning bath. He, too, was paying no attention to the battle of wills going on at the table, lost in the further adventures of the Green Lantern. While he read his comic book, he hummed a similar ditty to that of his grandmother.

Percy tried not to think about her son having inherited her mother's daffiness. Some things are better left alone. She reached up instead, and turned off the radio blasting the Andrew Sister's version of *Don't Sit Under The Apple Tree With Anybody Else But Me.* For an instant, silence reigned. Then everyone started to talk again.

"Sorry, Pop." Sera's voice was, however, devoid of any contrition. She tossed dyed blond curls. "But I have to get to the factory by eight and I won't have any time to polish my nails after work. I've got a big date tonight."

"How lovely." Mother spoke in a dreamy tone, the only one she used when awake. "So many young men you see, Serendipity, and nearly every evening. Have I met this new boy, what's his name?"

Sera didn't answer.

"She probably can't remember his name, grandma," Oliver said in a guileless tone, without looking up from his comic book.

"Out of the mouths of babes," muttered Percy.

Mother turned from the stove and dumped a large dollop of hot oatmeal into an empty bowl before an empty chair. Percy sat down and picked up a spoon.

"I'm in a hurry, Mother, so nothing else for me." Percy poured diluted, condensed milk over the warm cereal. She hated oatmeal and loathed canned milk, but neither eggs nor bacon had seen the inside of their kitchen in months. "Pop, I just got a job." She shoveled in a large spoonful of the cereal, trying not to taste it.

Everyone except Oliver turned and stared her. Money being tight and Pop unable to work with his broken leg, it left Percy to be the major bread winner of the family. They were having what President Roosevelt referred to as 'lean times.'

Pop was the first to speak. "What kind of a job? Is that what the phone call was about? You know, we don't take just any job." He raised his hand, pointing his index finger at the ceiling before making his further statement. "Cole Investigations has standards."

"Pop, it's a jeweler on Fifth Avenue. This Waller guy seems like a real jerk, but who am I to say no? Something about a dead elf left in his store window, and the cops are already there. It sounds in and out, but I did manage to get a two-day guarantee." She looked around at the rapt attention her remarks had drawn. "And, I'm making twenty bucks a day plus expenses."

"Twenty bucks?" Oliver looked up from his comic book, astonishment written all over his sweet, freckled face. "A day?"

"Oh, my," remarked her mother, doing her usual Zazu Pitts impression. "So much money! And for one day! Why, our rent is only nine dollars and we live here thirty days out of the month, sometimes thirty-one. Isn't that right, Father?" Mother stopped stirring the pot of oatmeal, turned, and glanced at her husband for support.

Used to his wife's zaniness, Pop looked at her and smiled. "It is, indeed, Mother."

"And in February, it's twenty-eight," murmured Sera, blowing on her nails.

Their parents had called each other 'Mother' and 'Father' since Percy could remember. Probably because Pop was named after Habakkuk, a biblical prophet. Mother's real name was Lamentation. With her willowy shape and long, white blonde hair, Mother looked more like a Dandelion, threatening to blow away at any moment.

Percy's family had a history of unusual, if not downright peculiar, first names on both sides. Her older brother's name was Adjudication, and no doubt the main reason he'd become a lawyer. So, stuck with Adjudication, Serendipity, and Persephone, the Cole off-spring was glad for the usage of nicknames, such as Jude, Sera, and Percy.

"I don't want you to put yourself in jeopardy on this job, not even for a king's ransom, Persephone." Pop turned back to his eldest daughter. "If I could go with you --"

"Don't worry, Pop," she interrupted. "Like I said, this should be in and out and the fastest twenty bucks - no, make that forty bucks – Cole Investigations ever made." She gulped down the last of her breakfast, got up, and took the car keys off the hook by the back door.

"Think Ophelia has enough gas in her to get me midtown, Pop?" The 1929 Dodge was the family car, old, black, and ugly, but its engine came to life each time you pressed down on the starter. The gas gauge was one of the many things that no longer worked, and between rationing and only being able to afford to put in one or two gallons at a time, father and daughter ran out of gas more times than they cared to think about.

"Put in five gallons, Persephone, right before my leg turned bad."

"That was two months ago." She gave it some thought. "Man, has it been that long?"

Pop smiled. "Nobody else driving it now except you."

"I would if Pop would let me," Sera interjected, with a pout.

"You got all those boyfriends to tote you around, Serendipity. You don't need a car." Pop's voice was kind but firm.

"Well, the last time I got home on fumes." Percy gave out a laugh and shook her head. "I'd better take the subway. It's faster, anyway." One thing about living on the lower eastside, a couple of blocks walk to the BMT and it got you nearly everywhere in Manhattan.

"Get off at fifty-seventh and Fifth." Pop talked as if she hadn't ridden the train a thousand times. "And good luck with the job."

"I'm taking your fedora, Pop. My hair's a wreck. Hope you don't mind." She snatched the hat off the rack near the back door then ran to the end of the table, reached over and tousled her son's short, damp hair. "You be a good boy and do everything Grandma says, Oliver. Don't forget your raincoat. And come straight home from school. Okay?"

He dropped his comic book and grinned up at her, the child who gave her life meaning. "Okay, Mommy." He screwed his face up, closed his eyes, and she placed a noisy, wet kiss on his forehead.

"You're just so yummy, I could eat you up just like a pistachio nut." Percy grabbed him in a bear hug and pretended to smother him. He giggled and so did everyone at the table. She left to the sounds of laughter.

≈

The Wives of Bath Press

The Wife of Bath was a woman of a certain age, with opinions, who's on a journey. Heather Haven and Baird Nuckolls are modern day Wives of Bath.
www.thewivesofbath.com